D1083358

IAN MACMILLAN

P·R·O·U·D M·O·N·S·T·E·R

NORTH POINT PRESS
San Francisco 1987

Printed in the United States of America
Library of Congress Catalogue Card Number: 86-62828
ISBN: 0-86547-279-3

Grateful acknowledgment is made to *MSS* magazine, the *Seattle Review*, *Literary Arts Hawaii*, *The Iowa Review*, *The Little Magazine*, the *Carolina Quarterly*, *Hawaii Review*, *Quarterly West*, *TriQuarterly*, and the *Missouri Review*, where portions of this work first appeared.

PROUD MONSTER

WESTERN POLAND, FALL 1939

First Engagement

In the low wood, his head bowed so that his line of vision to the long column of infantry is blocked by the lightly fluttering leaves in the foreground: Vyuko, thighs embracing the horse, his lance point on the ground to his right. In the distance, the powerful roar of engines. His commanding officer looks doubtfully around him. Panzers? Horses snort. Vyuko's flesh vibrates with the current of a hatred so potent that it feels like joy: They shall not reach the Vistula. He pats the horse's neck. Oh, beautiful animal, you and I will be the first to reach them. We will gather them on the lance like garbage! Like insects! The upper bodies of the men around him surge forward and back with the movement of their horses. The younger ones are frightened and shaky; the older ones are calm with resignation. And Vyuko, among the youngest, is incandescent with exhilaration. Vyuko, the first into battle; Vyuko, whose lance will be painted end to end with bright German blood. Down the line the order is called, and he lifts the lance, spurs, and feels the mighty flesh erupt under him. He shouts, aiming the lance at the now-scattering column. The wind presses his eyes; he knows by the sound of hoofbeats that he leaves his compatriots behind. His heart soars. Divine music.

In the tank, gripped with nauseating, claustrophobic fright: Richter, hands on the automatic, testing the turn—up, down, side to side the turret goes. Encased in his coffin of steel with the two men below him, he realizes that he is about to mess his pants, and the effort of holding it in is so great that sweat bursts from his face. The tank turns in a gasping jerk, throwing him against the housing. When he sees the enemy, the pressure overcomes his strength, and he feels it rush forth, then run like warm syrup down his legs. Cavalry, someone yells from below. Richter tests the turret again, aims. The slit is too small. Horses, lances, puffs of smoke, deafening noise, and then across his vision in a blazing flash a horse and rider. He lets off a quick burst, misses, and knows he is doomed. There is no surviving this; the magnificent forms of horses ripple everywhere, slick and powerful, vapor shooting from their snouts. There, there is one, coming straight and yelling. Richter pulls and cuts the horse from under the lancer, whose strange helmet flips in the air above his head. Gone.

In the low wood, Vyuko, sitting with his head resting on his crossed forearms. He weeps for his horse. So fine an animal, and to be ripped from under him by someone he could not even see. He hears the soft footfalls of other survivors and, in the distance, snorts of horses, but only a few. The rest lie slaughtered on the plain among the lances, soiled flags, men, overturned machine-gun wagons. Now steps, close by. A hand on his shoulder.

"Come, we must leave now."

"I have no horse. My horse is dead." Vyuko looks up. It is Jasiu, his pale and wrinkled face streaked with dirt. The old army man is an encyclopedia of tales about heroic exploits during the Bolshevik campaigns, and Vyuko is glad he is still alive.

"Come," the old man says, "we're going to regroup closer to the river. But I'd advise you not to go charging off after a tank next time."

"I hate them. They do not fight like men, and I hate them."

The old man looks at Vyuko, thinking. "I know," he says, "and you'll need that, because this is not 1920. This is different."

Richter, standing by the tank after having cleaned himself up. He looks at its shape, thinking. Behind him the other men laugh and poke fun at him for his indiscretion. He drinks water from a canteen, feels the cool air on his forehead. Then it hits him: What an invention! What a beautiful invention! Even the shape is sleek, artistic, and he is awed by the purity of its function. "Steel!" he says, and hits the side with an openhanded metallic whap. He goes to the other men and gestures with the canteen. "It is beautiful, no?"

"What?"

"That. It is beautiful. It is a beautiful device, a great invention."

"When did you discover this?"

"Just now. All the training, all the preparation, none of that struck me until just now. This is magic, magic!"

"Ah, you have confidence now?" one says. "Horizontal assaults we can handle. I trust we'll have no more vertical ones from you? You see, it's technically a form of sabotage."

The men laugh, Richter the loudest. "No, no more vertical ones," he says, "not while in a masterpiece like that."

"Good. We'll not tolerate such insults to our steel lady. And now we will drink to your coming of age."

Richter is abundant with pride.

CENTRAL POLAND, FALL 1939
Science

Professor Kluzak had been out on an ill-advised field trip with four of his favorite students when the Germans overran the town. So they had spent a cold night in the dewy woods, from time to time setting up the small telescope to observe the Germans' activities. But it was of little use because of its degree of magnification. To make the situation worse, the professor had run out of cigarettes, and his face had locked itself into a mask of frustrated desire and a kind of tragic wrath. Now it is late afternoon, and, as the professor leads the boys from one strategic position to another around the town's perimeter, he speaks often of the awkward position he is in, being Czechoslovakian by birth in a Poland overrun from one side by Germans and from the other by Russians. "This is complicated by the controversial nature of my publications," he says, and, despite their fatigue, three of the boys catch each other's eyes and smirk. They love the pompous, ridiculous old man and often pass time imitating him.

The fourth boy, Adam Kutrzebe, carries the telescope and speaks to no one. Just before the field trip, he was shamed in front of the other boys by the professor, who had discovered that Adam had soiled the microscope in a way so exotically nasty that the rest of the students had laughed for what seemed like hours. When no one was around, Adam had decided to test out something he had learned in science class. Sneaking around the empty classroom with a giddy, rubber-legged pleasure, he had gone into a storage closet packed with dusty beakers and jars and there had abused himself, depositing the result onto a slide. He was studying the awesome ranks of the bright little fish, like the vigorous larvae of frogs, when the professor had come in and asked him what he was doing. The old man had looked into the microscope and gone through a fifteen-second process of gradual recognition, the color draining from his face; then he had seen the residue oozing down onto the beautiful microscope's base. Now Adam lags at the end of the line of boys, the telescope on his shoulder. It seems peculiar to him that, in the awful shame of having been found out, nothing can compare with the visions he has of the lively micro-organisms and their myriad occupation of his own skinny body.

The professor stops and sits down on a rotting log. "This is pointless," he says. "Boys, if I don't get a smoke soon, I believe I shall lose my equilibrium."

Adam Kutrzebe wanders away from the rest, feeling he is not entitled to their company. He wonders why they can't simply go home; even if the Germans occupy the town, is there any reason why they will not continue to be able to sleep, eat, and read? After all, boys like himself could be of no use to the Germans. As he wanders, thinking, he rounds some bushes and sees in the distance a group of people doing something. Digging. Or perhaps not. He decides to tell the professor.

"Men?" he says. That means cigarettes. Suddenly the professor is excited and hurries toward the bush from which Adam had seen the people. But since the professor's eyes are bad, he has no idea what Adam is pointing out to him. "Get the telescope," he says. "Then we might know exactly who they are."

Adam sets the telescope up by the bush, pushing the feet of the tripod into the soft loam. He aims the lens on the group, trying to hold the scope steady, but is unable to fix it on anything he can identify. The professor becomes agitated, until he can bear it no more and marches off toward the group in the distance. At this point, Adam's eye catches something: the upper part of a human being, a man—Adam blinks, sees the still face with what appears to be a dark rose blooming on the cheek, and then he understands. Even through the thick, bluish haze between the group and the telescope, he can tell that they are bodies and that soldiers in long gray coats and German helmets are watching over men digging a hole. He runs to catch the professor.

Later in the evening, the professor sits and muses on the significance of what Adam has described to him. "My God, and for a cigarette I would have been in the hole with the other poor devils! Killing them! Why?"

"The thing on the man's face was a wound," Adam says.

"I tell you boys, the human race is afflicted with it—it is in our basic character! Duality! Superior, inferior, winner, loser, good, evil, Aryan, non-Aryan. We are obsessed with duality." The boys look at each other in the moonlight, wondering what he means. "I tell you it is genetic," he goes on. Adam blushes, hearing that word "genetic." That was what identified all those wildly competitive little sperms he had looked at. "In any case, we must stay out here until they leave," the professor says. "Find food some way. We cannot go back. I would not be able to bear seeing any of you shot."

"We can fight them," one boy says. "My grandfather has a shotgun. I can get it and we'll fight them and drive them off."

"A pleasant speculation," the professor says, "and it might come to that. After all, what *is* our neighbor to the west doing in our yard? In any case, your instincts are correct. We shall see."

The boys speculate on the question of how to get rid of the Huns, and Adam wanders off with the telescope on his shoulder. He sets it up and looks at the moon, which tonight shines down with an almost violent, phosphorescent brilliance. The craters are perfect in their definition, and the moon nearly fills the scope. He imagines walking in the craters, climbing from the beautiful shadows into the pale, white light.

Soon the professor joins him and looks at the moon with his naked eye. "Yes," he whispers, "this is a perfect night for looking at it. Despite everything, we still have the moon."

"It is three hundred eighty-four thousand kilometers away," Adam whispers.

NEAR LUBLIN, POLAND, FALL 1939
Travel Plans

Weitzman stood facing the three frightened children while his wife whispered harshly up at the side of his head. The German soldier was soon to be looked for, as indicated by the expectant look in his eyes above the huge gag of Weitzman's scarf. "Men disappear," Weitzman had said to the window. Now he stared somewhere above the children's heads, his face held in a mask of a kind of mulish objectivity.

"Is there any chance for us now?" his wife wailed. "How many times have I told you that you have to use good manners with them?"

Weitzman remained silent. The children looked at each other, wondering. It was, after all, the way he always acted in one of their arguments. It was their mother who always did the talking, and now that a certain normalcy had returned to the day, they began to feel less frightened. Their father was a huge bear with black hair reaching up in thick tufts above his shirt collar and growing in sawdust-clotted thickets along his forearms, and he was as silent as he was big. They had just witnessed what they figured was the first act of violence ever committed by the burly giant: When the German soldier, wearing a gray uniform and black boots that squeaked when he walked, had inspected Weitzman's papers and announced that he was to be relocated to a work camp to the east, Weitzman had reached out and folded the officer up the way a spider would a fly, easily containing his grunting resistance. Then he had tied and gagged him, using the scarf and a couple of belts. All the while, his wife babbled to the soldier in rapid, shocked apology. Then Weitzman had said, "Men disappear. I am not going with him."

The children waited. Weitzman gazed thoughtfully at the wall, and the German soldier repositioned himself to be more comfortable. "*Now* how will we get back in good standing with them?" she moaned, looking down at the soldier. "If we apologize, perhaps—"

"We are going south to the Tatras," Weitzman said. The children shifted on the couch and looked at each other. They had heard about the Tatras all their lives, and it was as if he had announced that they were going to Paradise.

"Oh?" their mother said. "And where will you get money for the train? Who will even *let* you on a train?"

"We are walking."

She went into a flurry of intense whispering: "Oh, of course! One foot and then the other. Children, too. Walk all the way to some mountains. Do you think I am insane?"

"I was born there," Weitzman said.

"Oh, is that so? I wasn't aware. You've only told me a thousand times. How can you expect children their age to walk hundreds of kilometers?"

"I carry stones all day. Logs."

"I am not going! I am going to figure out how to explain such ill-mannered behavior to them! We must make things right."

Weitzman remained silent. *Men disappear.* He could not shake the sensation that he was right. This time at least, he would not budge. He felt sad and embarrassed that it had come to this, but now, with the poor German all trussed up and staring at him, there was no way that they could stay. "We leave now," he said.

His wife folded her arms and looked at him with bewildered contempt.

"Each of you pack a grain sack," he said to the children. "Warm clothes, one extra pair of shoes. No toys."

"He doesn't really mean it," his wife said to the soldier.

Weitzman went into the pantry.

"We are poor Jews," she said to the soldier. "We are always frightened. Can you imagine how hard it is for us who have nothing?"

The soldier nodded. "After all," she said, "can you understand his obstinacy? He's actually a very gentle man, not a brute as he appears. He's a hard worker, too. You'll see just how hard one man can work!" The soldier nodded again. The room darkened a little as Weitzman's form blocked the light from the doorway.

"It's dusk," he said. "We are going."

"Well, have a safe journey," she said.

Weitzman left the room.

"Well," she said to the soldier, in a quaking voice, "it appears I must go, too! What a preposterous development!" She thought for a moment. "When we are gone, will you be all right? I mean, you will, won't you?"

The soldier nodded.

"Well, I'd better pack!"

She left the soldier, but he could hear her talking in the other room and then, later, outside. Not inclined to try to free himself yet, he sighed and wondered how he would explain his situation. He had known right away when he had seen the huge man that coming by himself had been a bad idea.

WESTERN POLAND, SPRING 1940
Sisters

Magda Iwanska looks out through the little bedroom window at the dusty road leading into the village center, while her eight-year-old sister Sofia stares thoughtfully at her back. "May I?" Sofia asks. Magda shakes her head. It is morning, and the Germans are gone. They had executed thirty men the day before, reprisal for the death of a soldier found in a dry well at the edge of the village. When Magda was ten, she had dropped a doll down that well, and she cannot drive from her mind the image of the soldier lying on it. She is now fourteen, and she feels uneasy about going to her grandmother's house because her uncle is lying in state there, waiting to be taken to the cemetery. She has never seen a dead man before.

"I knew it when you wouldn't take baths with me anymore," Sofia says. "May I, please?"

"No, stop it now. We have to go. Mother and Father expect us now."

"Just once?"

"No, I told you!"

Sofia walks away, her face gone red with bitterness. Magda watches her, then says, "Listen, we have to go now. I'll—I'll show you later."

"I want to see now."

Magda sighs with exasperation. "All right." She raises her woolen smock up to her shoulders.

Sofia stares at them, the full, rounded breasts with the brown nipples, each with little golden hairs around the edges. She draws in her breath with a long gasp. "They're bigger even than my fist!" she whispers. "Look, one has a little mole!" Magda lets the smock fall. "Wait, can I touch one?"

"No! What are you thinking?" Magda snatches her shawl off the bed and walks toward the front door, her little sister following.

Walking behind her sister through the village, Sofia watches the heels appear and disappear from under the smock floating just inches above the ground. She puts her hand inside her coat and feels her skinny chest. It's like a washboard, not even a ripple of fat. She wonders if she will be able to grow breasts like that, big rounded mountains with hard brown nipples—the most forward part of her body. She runs ahead three quick steps so that she can see Magda's chest in profile. Magda is looking to her right, at the church graveyard.

"Look at that," she says. Sofia looks. Men are pulling up the rusted iron fence at the back of it. "They have to make the graveyard bigger."

Sofia nudges her sister. "You know, I already saw them anyway. I peeked while you were sleeping. I just wanted to see while you were standing up."

But Magda isn't listening. They are nearing their grandmother's house.

Inside, their parents and aunts and uncles are drinking wine and talking in low, hushed tones. Their mother rushes to them, her face red from crying but twisted in anger. "Where have you been?" she whispers harshly. "The service is about to begin!"

"We forgot," Magda says.

"You forgot! My Lord, what were you thinking? Now go, pay your respects!"

Magda approaches the coffin with Sofia behind her, looks inside, and then goes to join her mother. Sofia approaches, looking down at the flat, foreshortened front of her body, and bangs the point of her hip on the lower corner of the coffin. The pain shoots through her like a flash of heat, and she forgets herself and lets out a sharp scream. They all look at her, and she stares at the floor. "I—I hit my hip. I only hit my—" They turn away.

Embarrassed, she looks into the box. He is dressed in his church clothes, and his face is a grayish white. Something is wrong with his forehead; they have put something in place of it—plaster. The huge, battered hands with the short black hairs on the fingers are folded carefully with each finger crossing another one. There is a smell, sweet but turned, like bad fruit. The lips are tight, crisscrossed with minute creases. When she studies the closed, puffed eyes, she feels a strange dizziness run through her, as if she is not standing on anything. She runs from the house.

Magda finds her behind the chicken coop. "What's the matter?" she asks softly. "What's the matter?"

"Was that him? Was he really dead?"

"Yes, the Germans shot him yesterday."

"Why?"

CENTRAL POLAND, SUMMER 1940
A Lesson in Language and Values

Reinefarth accepted the schnapps from Obersturmführer Müller, trying to recall how much they had consumed in the morning. But this was pointless; everybody was half drunk by noon anyway, and Müller usually led the way. Reinefarth found Müller repulsive, with his stubbled jowls and the series of urine stains on his pants fading the fabric day by day in subtle shapes, like a series of transparent map overlays.

Müller had summoned him to the trucks to discuss Reinefarth's "problem," which he was now hinting at with a kind of pompous jocularity. Reinefarth could not shoot men. He could not look into the pits at the grotesque tangle of bodies with their gaping, shattered faces. The first time he had tried, he had vomited on the ground in front of him, making an officer go ashen with speechless rage. Of course, you mustn't do this in front of the others, you mustn't humiliate yourself, your uniform. Reinefarth had settled after that into the sullen and rebellious attitude of an incorrigible schoolboy, but even this stance had become fatiguing, and he was bored with his perpetual shame.

"I have authority to shoot men who disobey orders," Müller said. "Here, have another." He filled Reinefarth's cup.

"I'd like to be sent back."

"You have a future here," Müller said, sitting down on the running board. "Why waste it? Going back has consequences. It is a thing that, once done, cannot be undone. Do you understand?" Reinefarth nodded. "But wait," Müller said, "I have prepared a little—lesson for you. Over there."

"I'd rather not."

"You must. It's an order. You must obey."

Reinefarth felt himself drift with growing drunkenness, so that everything, the trees, equipment, Müller with his urine stains, all seemed bright and two-dimensional.

Müller rose with some effort, as if testing his balance, and led Reinefarth past the trucks into the woods. It felt to Reinefarth like a dream, with the flat plane of his vision rocking and shifting in jerks. Soon he found himself standing in a clearing before a blindfolded woman who was tied to a tree. "Now then," Müller said. "Here we have your standard vermin, in this case a mute dolt who knows nothing of our, say, exercise here." Müller squinted at Reinefarth's face. "Are you all right?" Reinefarth nodded. "Look at the ground next to the dolt,"

Müller went on. Reinefarth looked, and focused on a rider's stirrup, and next to that an egg. On the other side of the woman was what looked like a little statue of a dancer. The absurdity of this arrangement made him reel with nausea.

"Please, shoot the egg with your pistol," Müller said.

Looking doubtfully at Müller, Reinefarth took out the pistol and aimed at the egg. Then he realized what Müller was up to. "I—what is the meaning of this?"

"The meaning?" Müller said. "Well, shoot the vermin then."

"I can't—I'm not going to shoot her."

"I don't understand."

"I can't."

"Can't what? Can't shoot an egg?"

Reinefarth sighed with exasperation. "Her. I can't."

"Where is 'her'?" Müller asked, his face a mask of exaggerated wonder. "I see no 'her.' I order you to shoot it."

"Please, I—shoot what? The egg?"

"It! It! The taller object in the middle!"

"Please—"

"I order you to shoot it!" Müller yelled. "Now!"

Shaking violently, Reinefarth raised the pistol, but, when it came to pulling the trigger, he could not. His hand began to tremble uncontrollably, and then his arm fell limply to his side.

His face florid with rage, Müller yelled, "You weakling! You poof! Shall I order a pink triangle for you, you poof?"

"I am not going to shoot it," Reinefarth said softly.

"I am through with you then," Müller said coldly, and walked back toward the trucks.

When Reinefarth returned to the trucks, he heard Müller talking to other soldiers about the incident. He was throwing his arms around and using the word poof. One soldier disappeared in the direction of the woman tied to the tree, and Reinefarth heard the single shot. After that Reinefarth walked away from the men, feeling weak with humiliation and bitter regret.

NEAR LUBLIN, POLAND, SUMMER 1940

The Collector

I had known Pervant in Kassel before the war, and that day, as the battalion entered the village, Pervant's place of exile for the past year, I sensed a nearly perfect completion of a process, and I thought, as I looked out over the green plains, it will be in some safe place, perhaps a dresser, in those same albums. I pictured Pervant years ago, holding the magnifying glass up and smiling with pride and a certain baiting smugness that had angered me. Pervant was to be hanged summarily, a confirmed enemy of the Reich. This was the business of the younger SS, robust and boisterous, who arrived in trucks, while I arrived in a limousine, my function administrative.

My heart rose in my chest when I saw him—yes, the records were correct. He was dragged from one of the larger houses by the soldiers, while his wife trailed behind, pleading in German. The difficult preparations for this day were the result of careful calculation: I had had to convince the regional administrators that Pervant was dangerous, a partisan involved in sabotage along with other members of the village. I walked the perimeter of the square as the portable scaffolds were erected, and an officer read a speech to the populace, the preface to the execution selections.

I entered Pervant's house. Yes, there was the old Victorian chair he had had in Kassel. The case, too, in which he displayed his collection of glassware—Murano, Meissen figurines, bright but worthless trash. Below the shelves were two drawers. I opened one, and the musty smell of old leather wafted up. It would be at the beginning of a section reserved for the British colonies, under British Guiana—my hands trembled as I flipped the pages, and there it was, the four-cent blue, 1856, *Damus Petimus—Que Vicissim*, a ship on a square of blue paper. Such fine, clear type, a nearly perfect specimen. I tore the page out of the album and folded it carefully around the stamp; the others in Pervant's collection were useless to me. Suddenly I was anxious for a leave from this dirty business, and my heart raced in my chest. I now had to protect the stamp until I could arrange a leave; it must not be stained, nubbed, or lost.

Outside, the executions were in progress; men and women swung under the single bar of the scaffold. Holding my hand over my pocket, I passed them on my way to my business. I would distribute leaflets detailing the new laws of the district until my fingers became dark with ink stains. I saw Pervant then, swinging from the middle of the scaffold, his mouth distended as if stuffed with food. Next to him swung a pregnant woman. One officer took snapshots of another, who leaned against the scaffold advising him about focus and depth of field without moving his mouth. I felt that everything was too confused, too chaotic, that the stamp would somehow disappear.

There was movement at the scaffold—the woman next to Pervant, her midsection. Across the fabric of her dress slid a soft lump that changed the shape of her pregnancy with a slow undulation. I pressed my pocket, afraid of the possibility of some accident, panic, gunfire. Feeling giddy and secretive, I returned to the car to open the page and study the minute printing of the ship, perfect lines under the dim, eighty-year-old pen cancellation.

My fears of losing the stamp were groundless. Inside of a month, I had it mounted in my collection, safe in the strongbox at home. But experience teaches us that nothing is complete. To my deep sadness, I discovered in consultation with an expert that the stamp is a forgery. The horror of it all is that I never will know if Pervant himself was duped, or had simply duped me.

KRAKOW, POLAND, FALL 1940
The Artist

The two women were passing by the painter and his easel on their way to the market. One of them stopped suddenly and then laughed softly into the palm of her gloved hand. "Look!" she whispered. They looked. The painter wore a black German uniform and little steel-rimmed glasses, and his hair was soft and very blond and fine. He was concentrating intensely on his work, the brush held up by his face with an almost feminine delicacy. Apparently he was doing a picture of the double-towered church at the edge of the square, and the women, standing a few meters behind him as he studied his subject, looked at one another with good-humored, speculative smirks. "So this is one of the Teutonic warriors," one whispered. "Look how small his feet are." His shoes were small, shiny, and narrow, small enough to fit either of the women. "My God," one of them whispered, "his shoes would be too small even for me!" and she had to clap her hand on her mouth to keep the laughter from exploding out.

"The hands," the other woman said. They edged a bit closer. As they had expected, his hands were very small and fine, like those of a woman, with professionally buffed nails at the ends of the fine-boned fingers. "He has the hands of an aristocrat," one whispered.

He heard them whispering and turned. "Bitte?"

Both women blushed and diverted their attention to the painting, which was half done: The sky and clouds behind the church and the foreground were finished in pinpoint photographic detail, but the dark twin spires of the church were still off-white holes in the rich painting. One woman cleared her throat. "It is very good—excellent work."

He said something they did not understand, smiling shyly, and then shrugged. They saw his face now—the thin nose and the large, liquid eyes made more liquid by the lenses of his spectacles; he had the face of a troubled romantic poet. He rose from his little stool, still smiling, and both women were surprised to see that he was above average in height and quite well proportioned. One woman nudged the other.

"Well," she said, taking the cue, "it's certainly fine work—you are a true artist." Now the full effect of his beauty hit both of them: He was like a god from a fairy tale, with his hair catching the sun, and his beautiful hands, and his black uniform with the twin lightning bolts on the collar. Then he spoke again in a strange, sandy, melodic voice, and seemed to be gesturing toward a café at the edge of the square. Tea. He was inviting them to tea.

One woman experienced a warm rush of wonder. Of course. After all, she was not married, and she suddenly imagined the process of his inviting her somewhere else, then some shy and romantically formal invitation to make love, and then she would hold that head of beautiful golden hair to her breasts, and with those beautiful hands he would—

He put his cap on. The peak was very high, and in the center, above his pink forehead and the gold cord on the visor, there was a little silver death's-head. Seeing it, she shuddered. She knew, of course, that they wore them but had never realized how high the peaks of their caps were nor how detailed was the glinting metal of the insignia. The cap made him seem too tall. He said something else, but she shook her head. "No, I couldn't. No, of course not. I couldn't. Thank you, no."

They left him and hurried across the square. "I didn't think he would be that tall," she said.

"Slow down. I'm almost running."

"I'm sorry. Let's get to the market. I just didn't think he'd be—"

"He was very handsome—how would you like to spend a weekend with a man like that?"

"I know," she said. "He was quite something."

But all she wanted now was to get away from him, to buy cabbage and bread and hot sausage and potatoes with dried soil still on them. And she thought, why on earth do they have to do that? Why on earth must they wear black and decorate themselves with lightning bolts and skulls, and why do they have to be so horribly and so repellently clean? She walked on, the little voice in her mind saying, monster! monster! into the image of his face.

NEAR POZNAN, POLAND, WINTER 1941
Father and Son

My cousin Jacek Kiel, a magistrate and militia volunteer during the roundup of the Jews, had a passion for watches. At first he had considered the solution to the Jewish question immoral; he had many friends who were Jews. But German authority could not be disobeyed, and Jacek had found that, because of his official position facilitating the deportations in our region, he could increase his collection by taking some of the finer watches possessed by the Jews. He became a vigorous worker in the deportations and ended up with a huge collection. He was, in effect, risking his life for these watches, since theoretically he was stealing from the Third Reich.

I happened to be in his house when the two SS officers and the guard broke down the front door. Paying no attention to me because of my youth and my somewhat dull appearance, they began slapping Jacek Kiel around, yelling in high-pitched voices that he was a thief, an enemy of the German people. They began pulling drawers out of the cupboard and dumping little mounds of gold and silver watches on the floor while he looked on, wincing each time he heard a crystal break. He began to whimper, reaching down and picking up one particular watch. "Look at this!" he gasped. "How can you destroy something so beautiful?" They looked—it was a tiny gold watch suspended in a sphere of glass. "Take it," he said. "My gift to you—we'll return these others with the promise that it will never happen again!" One officer held the sphere of glass with the watch in it close to his face and examined how the little gold posts leading out to tiny keys in the back seemed to be suspended in very clear water, and, as he turned it, the mechanism changed shape with a liquid undulation. "Paris," he whispered.

Jacek Kiel's father had been an extremely handsome man. The second SS officer saw his enlarged photograph on the wall, snatched it off its nail, turned it over, and took out a large quilled pen. "We are going to make an example of you, criminal," he said, preparing to write something on the brown paper sealing the back from dust.

The other officer cleared his throat and asked for the pen. Understanding his intent, the first one gave it to him, and he proceeded to write, "I am a criminal who has stolen from the German people." He wrote this in such a perfectly symmetrical and artistically beautiful script that even the man to be hanged seemed mesmerized by it. We all watched that line flow out of the tip of the pen, beginning with the large, florid "I," and I noted the look of rigid, almost furious concentration on the face of the SS officer.

My cousin swung under a branch of a tree, gently turning in the wind, with the picture hanging in reverse from his strangled neck. He stopped swinging when the rope froze, and stayed there throughout the early part of winter, until some townsman took the risk and cut him down, so that his body lay waiting to be claimed with the rope sticking out from behind his head, suspended horizontally like a thin stick above the brittle snow.

Few of the people remembered Jacek's father in his youth; his appearance had been almost a legend for years. While my cousin was still swinging from the tree, the townspeople used to go to the frozen form, snow and ice caked in the corners of the mouth and eyes, and they would furtively turn the picture over on his chest. Then they would stare for long periods of time at the extraordinarily handsome face of the hanged man's father.

BELGRADE, SPRING 1941
Flight

Imagine being suspended high above an immense drum that rolls slowly towards you. Sometimes, in flight, it is as if you are standing still in the sky while this drum turns, the features of its surface passing under you in pinpoint relief, sharp shadows marking each object. I am a crewmember in the nose of a Dornier, and it is April sixth. Below the stout vibration of man's greatest invention, the magnificent patchwork of the countryside inches under me. I am suspended inside what seems to me a diamond, its geometric planes around me forming an exact, crystalline symmetry. My heart floats high in my chest and awareness of life before this indulgence in pure beauty seems to me to have been coarse nonsense. No one dares face us! I need only to wait, encased in the forwardmost part of this product of high genius. Now I know that flight is the most valuable result of our long, stumbling, error-ridden struggle through evolution. Others may have discovered flight, but, in a device as artistically magnificent as this, I feel that we have created it.

There! Inching toward me, on the horizon of the drum, is a cluster of buildings, that, through the field glasses vibrating with the soothing rumble, melts magically into individual spires, bridge towers, and a church. The Dornier advances with a ponderous magnetism; the organs of my body are electrified with the purity of this soft movement, and they float inside my trunk almost sentient with exhilaration. It is April sixth—fixing a date seems for some obscure reason important. The cluster of buildings enlarges; it seems to rise to meet me and to spread laterally as buildings appear that were not visible before. I am amazed at the size of the city, aware that by tearing out its heart, we will spare a multitude of witnesses to all this. I will be seen—a tiny dot inside the polished diamond of the nose.

The city sweeps underneath me. There—that sensation of rising slightly: The bombs are being released. I must turn, contorting my body, to see them hit, squinting my eyes into oblique vision. There—exploding flowers. The smoke expands with a voluptuous, complicated shape: caught, it might look like the surface of a cauliflower; permitted to expand inside the outward-racing circles of shock waves, the blooms melt into one another until no building is visible, only a lumpy terrain of expanding smoke.

And then it is over. I must return to the world, remove myself from this crystal chamber, place my feet on ground again. I think of Plato—pleasure is unlimited, has no beginning, middle, or end. And this sensation of flight, once experienced, exists forever. No woman could ever give me this.

CENTRAL POLAND, SUMMER 1941
The String

Lekh Dielewicz would always be ashamed, humbled by the experience. His eighty-fifth birthday, and he was the man of the hour. He let himself go, held forth with a simple but effective speech about how one gets to last so long—yes, I drink, I smoke, I eat as I please—it's all a matter of the spirit. Many have died before reaching my age. It is perhaps only a matter of philosophical perspective. One lives if one *wants* to live. And hang restraint! It is a denial of life. I am eighty-five because . . .

After the party, his grandson yelled at him: You make this goddamned tortured speech about how one gets to be eighty-five! The boy's face was nearly purple with rage, and Dielewicz found refuge in his room; he sat there on the bed that still bore the impression of his dead wife's form and wept with shame.

And now the boy was dead. Dielewicz had assumed that this little gathering was partly for him, but, at eighty-six, he seemed to be in the unhappy position of commanding nobody's attention, except perhaps for the little children, who appeared and disappeared in his vision in a peculiar blur. His grandson had been killed by the Germans, and now the men gathered were drinking and talking in the parlor of his house after having sent their wives and children home. He had thought that some effort on their part would be spent consoling him, but they seemed interested only in the politics that had led to his grandson's death rather than in the death itself. Yes, he was a strong, intelligent boy, impetuous and fiery. Lekh Dielewicz remembered again the line of men, his grandson in the middle, his eyes locked in on his executioners, challenging them. Go ahead, the eyes said, I curse you for eternity! Then he was gone into that abyss on the edge of which Dielewicz had been for years.

Dielewicz rose from his chair and walked down the hallway to the parlor. The men turned. "Excuse me," he said. "Go on."

"Join us," one said, holding out a glass.

There was a strange blur of conversation; Dielewicz would find himself on and then off, as far as understanding its content was concerned—like an electrical light. Then he was talking: I cannot tell you how it feels for a man my age to lose his last grandson. What is there left, after all? So many have died before me, and he was the only one left. It is like a string that gets thin nearly to the breaking point, with one or two threads still hanging on—the family's regeneration, I mean. And that thread is now broken. Do you know what that means to a man my age? Ah, there is no experience worse than the loss of your children! At my age . . .

In an almost magical shift, he found himself alone, sitting in the parlor with a sticky glass in his hand. The house seemed to him gloomy and profoundly vacant. "I shall kill myself now," he whispered. He wondered why all the men had left, then found himself weeping. Yes, he would do it. "What is there left?" he asked. Then he thought, a belt around the neck, or perhaps a razor to the throat. The latter seemed best. He struggled up from his chair and went to the bathroom. The lamp was unlit, and in the darkness he waved his hand around slowly and felt for the glass chimney, then went to the little window and pulled back the curtain. The ground outside was bathed in cold, phosphorescent moonlight. He began to feel a little better. "Yes," he said, "I am the end of the string." Was there any point in suicide now? Time would remedy all of this quickly enough. "In any case," he said, "all life is sacred." As was his custom, he lit the lamp and shaved because he did not like to do it in the morning. Later he had a dream that was like a photographic negative. He was the only member of his family who had died, and they, bursting with health, shook his little house with their vitality.

WESTERN RUSSIA, SUMMER 1941
The Proposition

The body lies across a muddy track on the road of the German army's advance. The torso and head, without the helmet, rise just to the outside of the rut, and on the other side they can see the lower legs and boots, laden with mud thrown from tires and tank cleats. The middle of the body is driven into and has become one with the bottom of the track. Each time a truck rolls over the submerged midsection, the soldier's upper torso surges and seems to inflate, one arm rising slightly in a kind of fatigued salute. They can see little of the face because, except for the black gap of the mouth, it is shrouded in the heavy mud.

The boy and the girl sit inside the hollow of a clump of bushes, waiting for the columns to pass. At first they had been frightened that they might be seen, and they could not look at the soldier being run over, but now waiting to cross the road to return to their village had become so monotonous that the girl has become annoyed at the dust on her brown shawl and hair, and the boy, a school friend for years, has returned to a subject that always angers her.

"Our houses might now be in ruins," he says. "There's no way they'll see us, and this might go on for hours."

"So?" She cringes, seeing the soldier move under the tires.

"Please, listen. It's not as significant as you might think. Everybody does it. And look at you—you're sixteen, in—well, as the poets say, in the full bloom of youth. It doesn't even hurt!"

"Please stop it," she says. "This is tiresome." She picks at the shawl, looks again at the soldier. "Why don't they move him?"

"This is a war," he says, suddenly sounding distant and thoughtful. "It might go on for years, until nineteen fifty-one, nineteen *sixty*-one." Then he seems to explode with infuriated mockery. "And you—it'll still be there and past even letting little babies out!"

"Stop it!" she hisses. "You stop that! I told you until I was out of breath! It's against God's Commandment!"

"It's unnatural," he says miserably, "as unnatural as that down there, that man. Are you saving it for the worms?"

"I am saving it for my husband. Oh, there's a tank." They watch. The body surges up, then relaxes.

"Why don't you pretend I'm your husband?" he says. "I'll show you. It feels good. I mean it's what it was made for, after all."

"How do you know? Have you ever been with a woman?"

"N-no, I've been told about it though. Friends of mine."

"Hearsay. You tell me all this when you haven't done it?"

"I thought we could—well, both do it, just to see."

"No. It isn't right."

He moves closer to her, whispers, "Please, show me—it's almost dark now so I won't really see anything. Please, show me."

"No," she whispers.

"Will my eyes hurt you? Please."

"No."

He slumps miserably back on his knees and shakes his head. "For the worms," he says. "In the full bloom of youth and she is saving all this," and he gestures at her body, "all this, for some phantom husband. And it doesn't even hurt."

"You're being stupid."

He pauses for a moment and then overcomes his hesitation, reaches out, and puts his hand on her breast. She gasps and bats it away. "Stop that! My God, what are you doing?"

"It feels soft," he says. "I've never felt anything as nice."

"Don't you ever touch me like that again!" She looks down inside the shawl. "Look at that. You've dirtied my blouse."

"It felt heavy, too," he says. "It felt like it weighs a lot."

She glares at him with disgust.

"That is enough for me—I will take that with me all the way to my death."

The end of the column is in sight. "Why did you say that?" she asks. He doesn't answer, and watches the man. The last vehicles are two trucks and a half-track belching blue-gray smoke. They sway and slide in the muddy ruts. One, two—the soldier makes his weak salute, then settles; one, two. Then the half-track: one—and a long, surging twist, so that the head is briefly lifted from the mud. The trucks move on. Far beyond the trees across the road, the boy and girl can see billows of smoke rising.

"Fires," he says. "I've got to go home!"

"Why did you say that?"

He works his way out of the bushes and walks toward the road, looking each way for more soldiers. She follows, trying to keep her shawl from tangling in the branches. He is passing the dead soldier, and she begins to run to catch up; she is suddenly frightened and feels airy and weak. "Wait, wait." She cannot get her breath, and by the time she catches up with him she is crying.

"What's the matter?" he asks.

"Why did you say that?"

THE UKRAINE, SUMMER 1941
Welcoming Feast

He is fourth in line entering the village. His forearms and the heels of his hands are sore from the vibration of the motorcycle and from holding the rubber handgrips tightly. Everywhere there are sounds of the people's jubilation at being liberated from the Bolsheviks. Lining the road at the village entry are women in bright peasant costumes, waving scarves over their heads, and some men shaking squawking chickens at the passing vehicles. There is to be a feast. He knows that, with the immense distance they have crossed, crushing all resistance, his unit will lay over for the night.

A young girl with flaxen hair and striking endowments, despite her shortness, wraps a white scarf with rich blue embroidery around his neck. She has the exotic, slanted eyes of the Mongol. She wears a long, colorful skirt and an embroidered blouse, and she smiles up at him with a primitive joy. Behind him, he hears the sounds of chickens being slaughtered and wine bottles clinking together. The men of his unit have their tunics off and look unnaturally pale in the golden Russian sun. He takes his own shirt off, proud of the substantial, even heroic, proportions of his body. The women and girls of the village blush and giggle, and he marches toward the men of his unit.

Another motorcyclist in his unit, a fat man who has the tiresome habit of being too crudely scientific, says, with predictable technicality: I know fraternization is against the rules, but how would you like to pump the contents of your seminal vesicles into the belly of that little specimen? Frowning down at the crude pig, he says: Conquest, victory, love—why do you have to ruin this? Then he drinks, and little rivulets of wine course down his neck and collect in the hollows inside his collarbones. We are kings! he says. We do not "pump the contents" of anything! We fight, we liberate, we make love! Get away from me, vermin! The fat man laughs heartily and turns to the mound of greasy chicken piled up on an ornate table placed out on the soft grass of the pasture.

Dusk. He wanders unsteadily. He is drunk, but more with the sense of his magnificent achievement than with the sweet wine. Campfires dot the village perimeter. Peasant men and girls continue to serve the victorious army wine and cheese, hard wheat cakes, chicken, duck, and pork, and in the west, a violently beautiful strip of orange light lies along the horizon. I love this, he thinks. I love war.

It is as if fate itself rewards him: The girl of the scarf wanders near a small building, holding a fistful of little flowers to her face. This is perfect, he thinks. Nothing could be so perfect.

It is easy to beckon her into the shack. She speaks to him, smiling, but he does not understand. There is melody in her language. You have those eyes, he says. You have Oriental eyes. Checking once more for people nearby, he is amazed at the perfection of all this; no one is within thirty meters of the little building. So, he is alone with her. A subtle sheen of fragrant sweat glistens on her neck and shoulders.

He reaches for her upper arms and pulls her close, but she whirls suddenly in his grasp, and he has the large, soft breasts in his sore hands, and then, for a moment, he lifts her off the ground by her groin. Then she is gone. He calls after her, wait, wait, and there hovers around his face the delicate scent of her hair.

The next day, the heels of his hands are still sore from the motorcycle's vibration. Some of the previous night is denied him by the peculiarly short-circuited nature of his memory, but from time to time his fat compatriot laughs behind him and works on a song he is making up, about a pudgy, well-endowed peasant girl who has resisted the advances of a Hun. He sings on and on, at the top of his voice, adding lines that are ridiculously florid: Thus did the maiden bolt, leaving sweet air before the befuddled knight! Scratching his golden pate: Ah, why did fate this gem of procreation thwart?

Looking into the dirt road that his machine consumes kilometer by kilometer, he thinks, we are kings. We are kings. Then he yells behind him: Remind me to cut your head off when all this is over!

His fat friend laughs, and sings on.

THE UKRAINE, FALL 1941
A Photographer's Last Day in the Field

We had been out a month. None of them understood why I had to turn my back, hide, slip off to some quiet place to load it. Celluloid must be handled with great care, unwound only enough to hook it in, and the black door must be snapped shut immediately. I had to calm myself and try to make my hands obey me during this procedure; I returned, shining with sweat, holding the camera away from me like a deadly snake. Before my transfer, I had known nothing of this; I had ridden in bombers, scanning the distant patchwork of land under us and photographing bright flashes, expanding mushrooms that billowed with a voluptuous beauty, perfect circles of shock waves streaking outward toward all horizons. But on the ground it was different.

As always, the gaunt, unshaven corporal, a half-smile on his face, approached the empty house on a sneak with a kind of playful curiosity. The torch disappeared into the window and illuminated the room inside. Then the thatch began to take fire, the smoke curling heavily into the windless sky, like dye spreading slowly through water. So many houses burned that I did not raise the camera.

Behind the house, aged men with beards dug a hole under the casual gaze of soldiers. A mother and child stood and watched. The child did not cry. I approached on the flank of the soldiers, checking speed and depth of field. The mother lifted the child, knowing what was about to happen. The camera began to buzz in my hand, and I raised it just as the young corporal from Bingen lifted his Mauser to the mother's back and aimed. I saw this through the viewfinder, my finger on the release. Perhaps you have seen this picture. Behind the simple arrangement of people lies a vast, blank plain. I pressed and heard the sound, and shut my eyes. Later, when they were through, I sneaked off behind the burning house and vomited my rations into a dry cistern.

Up toward the little village, they had six partisans lying face down on the ground. They were tied up, and their heads strained up so that they could see the process of their execution. The gaunt corporal asked at which end he should start, and a discussion as to procedure ensued. Not understanding, the partisans muttered and whispered, apparently making plans to bargain. Finally, Oberleutnant Webber settled the discussion by taking out his Luger and approaching the men. I pressed the release six times, and one by one the heads flopped to the earth. When the last head dropped, I began to cry, gazing—my vision intensified by flooding eyes—at the evil device in my hands.

I rode back in a six-wheeled limousine. The officer in front held the camera, and I placed my hand on his shoulder and explained to him the rules of caution one must obey in handling such things. He agreed, turning it over in his hands and nodding thoughtfully. The car was like Heydrich's. Encased in the heavy, sleek machine, I felt safe for the first and only time we were in Russia.

LVOV, POLAND, FALL 1941
Street Cleaning

Obersturmführer Fischer sits at the table at the edge of the square, looking into the pale amber wine. At his side, his aide Heppler laughs as he watches the proceedings, Fischer's idea, which Heppler had called "first prize for inventiveness." The tablecloth balloons in the breeze, and Fischer notes that the heat of summer has finally passed, which should make his job of eliminating the city's ubiquitous vermin nearly tolerable. Across the table, out in the square, his men peer down the muzzles of their rifles at the hunched backs of perhaps a hundred Jews. Before being relocated to the Janowska camp, they are cleaning the stones of the square with their tongues. The only resistance was taken care of an hour before, when a young man refused Fischer's order and got his head cracked by the handsome young soldier who now struts around the perimeter of the cleaning crew, lightly slapping his truncheon against his thigh, saying, "Good! Excellent! You! You missed a spot, you idiot! You'll be punished for such sloppiness!"

Heppler laughs again. "Our friend struts like a rooster, no?"

"He has a weakness for these women," Fischer says. "His only fault. Where is this wine from?"

"Oberwesel."

At the near edge of the group, Fischer sees a boy who, unlike the others, seems to have become fascinated with his work. He pauses, looking at the flat stone, spits, then continues licking. Heppler sees him, too, and squints. Curious about the boy's lack of inclination toward the backward glance or moan of protest, they lean forward to observe him more closely. "A dolt?" Heppler asks.

"It is likely. They are all dolts of one degree or another."

Born deaf, the boy has experienced all with a clarity of vision exaggerated by silence. Assuming that they were involved in some enforced but necessary rite, that the men of the black uniforms were perhaps priests imposing their harsh penance on them, he had obeyed the frightened language of his father's face and had begun to lick the cool stone. Gradually he had worn the surface dirt away, and there had emerged before his eyes a jagged vein of white embedded in the gray. Deep in the white there was a finely fractured translucence that riveted his attention: It was warm ice, the winter season suspended in stone, and it struck him as he revealed it—a diagonal line dividing like the branch of a tree—that he would never forget the smooth, pale transparency that disappeared down into itself, or the fine, glistening cracks, or the sheets of parti-colored brilliance with the points of blue and green light.

"I've had enough," Fischer says, sighing. "Order them to the camp."

Spitting and wiping their mouths, the Jews line up for the march to their new and last home. Fischer sees the boy looking back toward the square with a dumbstruck expression, as if none of this could distract his attention from the stone he had licked.

As they are marched off, Fischer crosses the square, feeling strange, as if the ground where the Jews had licked the stones might drop out from under him at any moment. He is suddenly uneasy; he no longer enjoys his jest. He stops at the boy's stone, leans over, and studies the vein of quartz. After a few seconds, his mind becomes suspended in a ticklish half-memory, as if his brain were clumsily laboring at recalling something important, like a familiar but forgotten name. Then he thinks, I must go home soon. This infernal business. I must go home.

"Are you ill?" Heppler asks from behind him.

Fischer stands and is dizzy, so that spots of light sweep across his vision. "No," he says. "No, it must be the wine. It makes me homesick. It is very good, no?"

THE UKRAINE, FALL 1941
About Face

The three of us were drunk as usual, on spirits confiscated from the executed. First there was Matthes, whom I thought of as "the poet" because he fancied himself an intellectual and this, his stint in Einsatzgruppe C, an adventure for a man of refined tastes. During our conversations, he would jot down notes in a leatherbound journal. Then there was Kohler, new to our drinking group, a large man who spoke rarely and was given to black moods. Then myself, an Unterscharführer like Kohler.

This evening I watched Kohler in his moody indulgence, gazing into his schnapps while Matthes talked on about literature in the new

Reich. I knew what was troubling Kohler. Our function, normally, was to oversee the administrative work connected with the liquidation of village populations in the Ukraine; the liquidation itself was carried out by Waffen SS, executing people in threes into tank ditches using small-bore rifles and PPKs and shooting them in the back of the neck. Because of a troop shortage, Kohler had found himself in the position of shooting these Jews himself and had whispered to me after the first long day, "My finger is sore—my finger is sore! The tension, I think. But we killed thousands today!" Then I said, "Eight hundred and six." He blinked, surprised at this number. After two days of this detail, he had retreated into silence and had begun to drink more.

But tonight the tediousness of the poet's speech exasperated Kohler out of his silence. The poet was looking up from his notebook, saying, ". . . so this is why double meanings seem to me degenerate, yet I can't resist—"

"Necks!" Kohler snapped, heaving himself forward in his chair, "write something intelligent for me about necks, you who see double—your, your deeper vision, your abstractions! Tell me about necks!"

In the evening gloom of our billet, a peasant house in a liquidated village, there was a silence through which the poet grinned at Kohler with good-humored contempt.

"If you are wondering why the neck," I said, "it is that the place of entry one inch below the occipital point of the skull ensures that the bullet will not ricochet and that there will be a minimum of pain to the patient—I mean—"

"Patient!" the poet roared. "Patient! Mass, you're a genius! May I steal that from you?" He lifted his glass to me, laughter taking his speech away.

"An error," I said. "The liquor, it—"

But the poet couldn't stop laughing, until tears filled his eyes and he spilled some of his drink over his knuckles.

Kohler's anger had now turned into a kind of benevolent disagreement. "Necks have personalities," he whispered, placing his hand on the poet's arm. "Walking to the pit, their hands covering their private parts, they are faceless." Then his eyes became bright. "But when they turn to the pit, and I aim at that spot, I see a special face, one with more expression!"

The poet stared at him, thinking.

Kohler whispered, "Red ones with those deep, horizontal creases, farmers' necks, I believe. Then necks that are tubular, whose vertical muscles have no definition, so the target is in that fine point of hair? Or boys with soft down, sometimes as blond as Heydrich's? Moles, scars, errors in grooming. You see, when they look down, the angle accentuates it, like an upturned face!" Kohler nodded excitedly, making it seem that the poet obviously should agree with his discovery.

"Look!" Kohler said, turning in his chair. "Look! My neck is long, my entry point a deeper hollow under—"

"Stop," I said.

"I used a mirror," he whispered, his eyes bright with growing lunacy. "I studied it in a mirror. What do you think, O spinner of abstractions?"

But the poet seemed not to be listening to him. He stared at some point in the middle distance between Kohler and myself, his face pale and without expression.

LENINGRAD, WINTER 1941

Stew

My father has now broken the couch up and is carefully scraping the dried glue into a can, using the pocketknife he usually uses to open letters. Mother has a pot on a wire grate over the sink because there is no fuel for the stove. In the sink she has a little fire going; she fans the smoke out of the window, and it comes back with each stroke, as if rocking. On the floor there are two green felt Saint Nicholas dolls, now ripped open and empty; we will stuff them with paper. Next my father will scrape the wallpaper in Peter's room. Last week Mama wrapped Peter in a sheet, and we took him to the church and left him by the graveyard. There was ice in the corners of his mouth and eyes. Our boots squeaked on the snow. Mama laid him next to an old lady with bare feet, who was wrapped up in frilly window curtains.

The pot splutters in the sink, and I can smell the odor of petroleum jelly. Mother put that in first, then sawdust, and then the beans from the Saint Nicholas dolls. Across the room, my grandmother sleeps on a cot. She is so thin that the blue veins on her arms can be held away like tiny, soft pipes under her skin, and she smells like old food or the toilet. She does not speak, and Mama says it will only be a day or two before we take her to the church.

The wallpaper makes hard chunks of whitish stuff that smells almost sweet. Mother takes spatula loads of it to the pot and shakes it in, and the sweet smell replaces the smell of the jelly. It is getting dark now. We will eat soon and have to hurry because we have no candles.

While we eat, I see that Grandmother is watching us, blinking and moving her mouth. Mother sighs and looks at my father, who shrugs once, trying to swallow the stew. Then he says, "No, it's too late for her." My grandmother blinks.

In my room I peel thick, dry paint flakes from the windowsill and eat them. The flakes have three thin layers of color: white, green in the middle, and light gray. I set my dolls up in their house. The small mother doll with the porcelain head is very old, once my grandmother's. She wears a peasant costume. The boy doll wears shorts with straps and has no shirt. Father will not take the glue from the little bed and chairs and the wardrobe because there isn't enough for the stew. The insides of the dolls are hair, so he won't need that. I speak to the dolls in a whisper because my parents think I am sleeping: Shh, don't worry, the bombers will be gone soon. Don't cry. After a while, I think that Peter is in the room. A picture of him, like smoke, moves in the darker corner. I decide that the little boy doll is Peter. He sits in the chair in the living room next to the mother, his arms down at his sides like at the church. Peter gets up and goes to the window to see the planes. Get away from there! Mother snaps. I'll spank you! Peter stays at the window, and Mother strikes him. He goes back to the chair crying. Wait till your father hears of this! The house shakes as the bombs fall. The iron frying pan in the kitchen falls off the counter, and Peter is now off the chair and on the floor, lying on his face. Mother picks him up, puts him back on the chair, and waits for the planes to go away.

Then the wardrobe falls down in front of Mother, and she gasps in dismay. How will she pick it up? Peter, help me with this. It's so heavy and I'm only a girl. Peter lifts the wardrobe back up. Mother looks at him and then says, Peter, thank you, would you like some candy? Yes, I would, he says. She goes to the kitchen, past the frying pan, and brings it out. Peter is sitting now with one hand up, holding the candy. Can I have some, too? Why, yes, Mother says, of course you can. The white flakes of candy sting my mouth at first, and then I taste the sugar. Oh, this is good.

Yes, it is, isn't it? she says.

Can we have more?

And she says, yes, all you want. There's plenty in the kitchen.

NEAR SMOLENSK, WINTER 1942
Philosophers

Sheltered from the caustic and torturous wind Privates Heiberling and Wirtki huddle under the thin woolen blanket, suspended at head level and draped over their helmets. Their shelter is built in an icy ditch and framed by two frozen corpses bridging the banks. One body is that of their commanding officer, the other of a young private from Hamburg. Both men frequently lapse into that sleepy half-consciousness that they know is the gateway to death, and they must prod each other awake. Heiberling has an advantage; he is kept awake by a sharp pain in his knee, injured when he fell on the dead officer and, with the full force of his weight, hit the knee on a stone-hard buttock. He is afraid that the cap is cracked.

With awkward, labored speech, using lips that refuse to obey the mind's order, Heiberling says, "I must keep moving my toes. I must concentrate on my feet." He pauses, moving his legs. In this cold, movement of any kind is agonizing; it permits the cold to seep viciously through their clothes. "Anyway," Heiberling says, "the meaning of all this is clear. Nations are like single persons. Composites of all the possibilities of personality."

The tent fogs with his breath. He looks up at the bright points of light in the blanket—holes through which light shines with a violent brilliance. "We contribute to one part of its personality," Heiberling continues, "but we must bear the consequences of all those other features, the demonic aspects. We have overreached." He pauses, looking at Wirtki. "What do you think?"

"My mind is too numb for philosophy."

In the ensuing silence, Heiberling looks up at the dim form of his commanding officer's frozen thigh.

Wirtki clears his throat, shaking himself from his frigid stupor. "We haven't a chance. We're dead."

Heiberling shakes himself, moving his limbs to test their feeling. "Someone will find us. The Russians are as closed out as we. No danger. Besides, visualizing the deeper meaning of all this keeps me awake."

"I am visualizing my death," Wirtki says. "I visualize a world without me. I see now that the progression of events I would be responsible for will not happen. The world will be inevitably different. My wife marries someone else, his genes follow into the future rather than mine. Do you see?"

"That is an interesting thought. But you are not married."

"I am speaking of the woman who would be my wife. I have had only one woman, and only once."

This surprises Heiberling, who has had no women at all. But he decides against mentioning this.

"I see no grief," Wirtki says, "just the simple fact that Paul Wirtki was but now is not. He had memory, his own little infinity of experiences, his unique character like none other on the planet, a face that, once known, could be distinguished from all others on the planet. I see a world without that. A world devoid of me."

"Yes, an interesting thought," Heiberling says. "But have you no room for optimism?"

"No."

Heiberling shakes himself, looking at the dim profile of his friend with the blanket draped over his helmet, next to the young soldier's frozen legs.

"The fact that people will remember me is irrelevant," Wirtki says. "I can remember people, too, but not their secret minds. That dies with me. I see a world without that mind." His head sags on his knees. Then, in a muffled voice, he says, "This mobile package of flesh no longer exists."

Later, as the wind howls above them and the points of light in the blanket die out, there is a period of sleep. Perhaps it is night, but Heiberling's pain wakes him up once more. He cannot feel anything from the injured knee down to his feet. Soon he realizes that the subtle radiation of warmth from Wirtki is no longer there, has fled upward into the bleak Russian sky. Putting his head in his hands, Heiberling understands that he is alone. He pauses, looks up. "I've been thinking," he says, "we describe death as a condition. This is wrong. Only life is a condition. Technically there is no death." He stops, thinks, then says, "A corpse is inert matter, like a pile of stones." He sighs with fatigue, wondering how long it will take. "You know, I have had no women. I have had none at all. But, after all, I am only nineteen."

RAVENSBRÜCK, SPRING 1942
Giving Birth

Marte Dekker waits for the young Polish woman lying on the dirty mat in the corner of the treatment room to give birth, and she glances frequently at Luise Schmidt, who runs water into a deep sink. Schmidt isn't feeling well today because she and her lover, an SS information officer, got drunk together last night. Schmidt has heard rumors of his infidelity and has spent the morning taking it out on prisoners, particularly the seamstresses in the block she commands. She has beaten two of them black and blue with a section of metal cable, her favorite weapon. One is so sick that she will probably be put out of her misery with an Evipan injection. And now this surprise stint in the hospital is further annoyance for her; she is not a nurse, and attending abortions and disposing of the newborn are tasks she feels are beneath her.

The Polish woman cries out, twisting the front of her smock with white-knuckled fists. Marte observes that the monstrous belly has flattened: The baby is in the birth canal. She leans down to the sweating woman and nods, then balloons out her cheeks in a parody of straining to push. Blearily, the woman comprehends and pushes until her face is nearly purple with the effort.

Schmidt stands at the sink, eyeing Marte. "Where are you from? The country?"

"Near Kassel. A hundred kilometers west."

"Ah, peasants aren't given to lying. Then tell me"—the woman screams, then pants heavily with loud, hoarse growls—"what you've heard."

Marte blushes, angered that Schmidt would call her a peasant. She wants to say something, but Schmidt is connected to power. One insult and she would be a prisoner.

"I didn't hear anything in particular, only that—"

The tone of the Polish woman's growling has softened into moans of release, and she now lies pale and sweat-drenched. Marte pulls up the smock; the baby is out, lying between the blood-streaked thighs, still attached by the even corkscrew of cord. It is a boy, slick and pink and patched here and there with a yellowish material. It moves slowly, arching its back.

"Come on, what have you heard? Tell me and I can do you a favor."

"Please," Marte says, and puts on rubber gloves, "we must attend to her. She must be back at the plant tomorrow."

She quickly cuts the cord and lifts the baby. Its mother cannot see its sex. Schmidt laughs, and walks over to her, and extends an index finger from her own waist.

"Tadeuz," the woman moans, gazing at the ceiling. "Tadeuz."

Marte puts the baby into the deep sink, immersing her own arms nearly to her elbows, and places the heavy screen down in the water. Pinned on the bottom, the baby moves, slowly thrusting out its legs and arching its back. Like all prisoners, the Polish woman has heard of this ritual and knows what is happening, but she gazes at the sink with longing, her face suddenly radiant with pride. "Tadeuz," she says.

"What have you heard?"

"Only that the new administrative—"

"Secretary! Yes! That little slut!"

Schmidt backs toward the door.

"The two of us should clean this immediately. The—"

"You clean it. This isn't my work," Schmidt says, her face twisted with anger, "not for someone like me!"

"Pig," Marte says softly to the departing figure. She removes her gloves, smiling, feeling a little better. She hears faint sounds from the sink—the screen scraping against the sides. The Polish woman stares at the ceiling, her hands clasped under her chin and her face still held in that odd look of exultation.

NEAR THE WESTERN BORDER OF POLAND, SUMMER 1942

State Visit

Running his eyes along the deep V-shaped trench cut into the plain, Stefan stands at attention, trying to control his nervousness. The sweat from his hands makes the stock of his .98 slippery. Next to him, Klaus seems calm, gazing over the plain at the line of trucks and at the billows of dust hovering over the road. "Stand at attention," Klaus whispers. "He is coming now." Oberleutnant Faber shouts toward the trucks, and the first group is herded toward the trench. The riflemen stand at attention above the ditch, not averting their eyes toward the six running men, all wearing dark suits dusted by the trip to the place of execution. The last man in line crawls into the trench, blinded by tears and panic.

"Apparently he wants the executions to be in progress," Klaus whispers. It is so. The order is given, and the line of men pitches forward, their heads snapping from the powerful impact, creating around each a brief, luminous globe made of tiny droplets of sweat and brain that catch the light just before the bodies fold into the trench. Sweating, Stefan tenses himself at attention and fixes his eyes on a dark spot of urine spreading in the pants of the dead man nearest him.

Reichsführer Himmler arrives in an open-topped limousine. He greets Faber, nods to the guards and riflemen. He is close, his uniform shining, the black leather squeaking as he moves. Stefan follows him with his eyes, his heart beating. He is surprised that Herr Himmler is so soft faced, so average looking.

Reichsführer Himmler is jovial, even excited about the proceedings. He studies the dead men in the trench, then turns and nods to Faber, who yells in the direction of the trucks. Six men, again all wearing black suits dusted by the trip, run slowly toward the trench. They must climb over the bodies of their comrades. Before putting his back to the riflemen, the man closest to Himmler looks up with a brief, sheepish glance.

Klaus clears his throat and whispers, "He should stand back. He is too close." Faber raps out the order, and the heads snap forward, flashing those quickly expanding halos in the sunlight, and the men fold into the ditch in the echo of the Mausers. And there is another tiny sound, a double splot of something wet landing. Reichsführer Himmler looks down at his uniform at the small pieces of bone and brain on his shirt and clinging to the brilliant leather of his boot. Suddenly his eyes glaze, and he seems to lose his balance momentarily. He turns, stunned, and reaches out for support.

"Do not break rank," Klaus whispers harshly.

"But Herr Himmler is ill," Stefan says.

"Do not break rank!"

Herr Himmler is helped back to his limousine. Faber kneels before him and wipes the bits of hair and brain off his boot, while the driver whispers to the shaken man, his hand on his shoulder. Herr Himmler climbs trembling into the limousine. The executions continue. The receding billows of dust cut the monotony of the horizon.

THE UKRAINE, SUMMER 1942
Four Women

"He is very proud."

"I know."

The two women sit close to one another, heads bowed over bowls of peas, while across the room the daughter and deaf grandmother sit separated by a small, ornate table. The grandmother knits quickly, so that the needles look like beetle's feelers waving over the bright yarn.

The mother leans up from her chair, looks out through the little four-paneled window at the village road. The daughter's knee begins to jounce with a rapid rhythm that makes the teacups on the sideboard rattle, and the mother glares at her. She stops.

"The Germans like him, he told me. They're so shorthanded with the militia that they plan to keep him on for weeks."

"Are they—" The visitor turns and glances at the grandmother and daughter; although the girl is fifteen, she is still a child.

"It's all right. Katya's known about it. Everyone knows about it. Poor Granny wouldn't care anyway—she's a little, well, you know, senile. She still treats Katya like a three-year-old." She pauses, thinks. "Yes, they're killing the Jews. All of them. Into tank pits." She leans up, looks through the window. "Ah, here he comes now. He's carrying something, probably from the—you know, spirits, trinkets, little things they let him keep. See the armband?"

"Yes."

"He is very proud of it."

"I know."

The teacups and saucers begin to rattle again, and the mother glares at the daughter. She stops.

"It means opportunity," the mother says. "We're safe now from the Bolsheviks, and he is interested in a position with the Government General. The Germans, of course"—she looks around at the daughter and the grandmother, thinking—"that is, the Germans—they'll leave us alone and protect us from the Russians. As for the Jews, well—"

"I'm not going to complain."

"Nor I. Here, let me get the door."

She places the bowl of peas on the windowsill and opens the door for her husband, who enters at a fast walk, sighs quickly, then lets his eyes adjust to the dim light inside. He says, "What a day! I tell you it's amazing, amazing!" Then he places his sack on the floor behind the door and removes the white armband with the militia insignia stenciled in black ink on one side. The daughter watches with bright curiosity.

"And where did you work today?" the mother asks. The daughter's knee begins to jounce, then stops.

"Everything happens so fast," he says. "Polny, just an hour's walk."

The daughter is suddenly very still. In a high, unnatural voice she says, "Polny? All of them?"

"Yes," the father says, not looking at her.

"Shall we look in the bag?" the mother asks.

"All?" the daughter asks.

"Here, more spirits," the father whispers softly, as if he barely believes it. "This is a cordial from Vienna."

"Cordial?" the daughter says. Then she stands and walks rigidly through the doorway to another room. From there they hear a high, soft wailing.

"What's the matter with her?" the father asks.

"Nothing," the mother says, and then softly, to the visitor, "She will get over this." The father does not hear. The three of them look inside the bag, tipping it into the light from the window.

When they are finished, they notice that the grandmother is no longer in the room. The mother tiptoes to the hallway and sees her sitting in the bedroom with the daughter on her knees before her, face buried in the old woman's lap. The old woman rocks her slowly, staring at the even part in her hair. "Is it your stomach?" she asks. The daughter nods. "Well, that's too bad. Let me think. Perhaps a story." She strokes the daughter's hair. "Here: Once upon a time there were two brown rabbits. . . ."

NEAR BIAŁYSTOK, POLAND, SUMMER 1942
Useless Knowledge

Pfoch realizes that Sturmführer Weiss listens to his story with an attitude of insolent, patronizing contempt, but he wants to go on anyway. Weiss is the only audience available. Pfoch sips his wine, then leans back in the porch chair of the village police station. Weiss, of course, is too young to understand. "We were to shoot them all, and the Gypsy tribe had seen too much. That's when I saw her. The thought of her blindness was perhaps the most intriguing thing. I mean, she—"

"You told me that," Weiss says, then sighs and looks away toward the thatch houses in the village center. "In fact, you said you would break the rules and partake of the—what was it? 'Magnificent endowments of the Gypsy bitch,'" and then he laughs with annoying force, apparently at the thought of Pfoch's wording, and trails off into a series of snorts, like a pig. "I saw her, too. Ridiculously healthy, I'd say. In fact, one of our younger guards picked up her skirt a little to take a closer look at those endowments—with an ass like that, I wondered if she would be too much for a pious old fellow like you."

Pfoch bristles with anger. "Anyway," he says, trying to maintain his composure, "I took her to my quarters, chained her to a beam, and went back to work. Technically, Gypsies are almost legal for the satisfaction of sexual need. They are, after all, of pure blood. Himmler himself is said to be interested in this phenomenon." Pfoch pauses while Weiss smiles with condescending scorn at the thought of Himmler. In the distance, beyond the amber thatch roofs, there is an explosion, and they wait to see the first billows of smoke, which rise into the windless air beyond the church. "So at sundown I went back. If you can believe this, I saw that she had been gnawing on the beam where I had wrapped the chain."

. . . In the room stands Pfoch considering how to do it. Because of his nervousness, he feels no sexual arousal yet, although she stands there in all her uncivilized beauty looking in his direction, sweat trickling down from her neck into the rich cleft of her breasts revealed in the folds of the colorful Gypsy blouse. He imagines the powerful curves of hips and buttocks, now only suggested under the long skirt, and she looks clean, not a blemish on her dusky skin. It is all his to do with as he pleases, and nothing, not the day of killing, the suspicious reports of losses in the East, none of it can intrude on the awesome pleasure of knowing he is soon to enter that hot, animal flesh. He knows of the refinement of the senses of the blind, and as he moves silently, she follows him with her eyes, listening. Pfoch approaches, knowing from simple domestic experience with his wife that, despite lack of arousal, despite his fatigue, the contact of searching hands in soft, yielding flesh will overcome his resistance. . . .

"She bit me, not hard, but hard enough to make me stumble back." Weiss laughs, then belches with lazy satisfaction. Pfoch is amazed at his thoughtless assurance. "I experienced impotence," he says. "It's true—regardless of the opportunity. The blindness fascinated me, too. Do you know what I mean? Somehow blindness heightens the sensation of sexual possession. But I was impotent."

. . . Pfoch is disgusted, angry, hurt. He walks to the wall where his tunic and belt hang, removes the automatic from the holster, and is startled to discover that it still feels warm, although he had discharged it into the backs of a hundred necks hours ago. He slides the sleeve of the automatic back, forward, and her attitude changes. In the primitive arch of her eyebrows, he sees a calm resignation. She looks directly at his face, and he sees two vastly dilated pools of a deep and liquid blackness, like wells. She seems to see him for the first time, in fact looks through him at some unknown distance behind. He points the pistol and feels his body stiffen with a familiar anticipation. . . .

"Did you shoot her?" Weiss asks.

"No. Later I took her out to the holding area and left her there with the others for the next day. Perhaps some other officer got her, I don't know. But by now she's under the ground." Pfoch leans back, thinking. "Then I understood it. Do you know that sensation you get just before you shoot someone, when you tense? Then after, that rush of, well, a kind of weak-kneed giddiness? I realized that impotence isn't what it seems to be."

"You think too much," Weiss says, laughing.

"I knew it really when I threw the sleeve of the automatic. What you have is potency finding a new residence."

"My friend, I think the remedy for your philosophy is another glass of wine." Weiss pours, and Pfoch looks angrily at him. He knew it all along: Young men know nothing about themselves.

"All this shooting," Pfoch whispers, "is oblique rape."

"Oh, God," Weiss says, "you tire me out. Listen, come with me tomorrow; we'll do what a friend of mine and I do every few days. We get a couple of girls, young ones, you know? We take them to our billets, we make them do everything. If they squawk, we beat them, tie them up, whatever. We make it last four or five hours, we use them up. Do you understand? Their pretty little 'endowments' get used up." He laughs with that irritating force again and trails off into the disgusting series of vulgar snorts. "You come with us," he says. "You come with us—your little worm will stand up like the barrel of a rifle, I promise."

"My God, you know so little about yourself, so little."

Weiss smiles with impudent fatigue. "Well, what use is knowing about yourself, after all?"

STALINGRAD, FALL 1942
The Pig Who Understood

Semyon Lubko looks out the window again. He and Nikolai Polyonov are on watch at the edge of the tractor factory. Their orders are due to come down in less than an hour, and Semyon Lubko's face is twisted with fear and a kind of dumbfounded wrath. No one had expected the fighting to be like this, where bomb by bomb and bullet by bullet the city was being reduced into piles of bricks and twisted metal. No one had expected 70 to 80 percent casualties, or to stumble around a corner and stand face to face with German soldiers, or to have to fight them with thumbs gouging eyes, or to smell their acid sweat and their blood. Lubko positions the Degtyarev on the windowsill and shakes his head. It is obvious to him now that he will not survive this, and he considers deserting.

Nikolai Polyonov clears his throat softly and looks at his comrade. "I am curious to see our orders," he says.

"God Almighty," Lubko whispers, "I think the strategy is to suffocate the Germans with an avalanche of flesh! We throw ourselves at them by the thousands! I see—we'll exhaust their ammunition with our bodies! Ah, what brilliant strategy!" He is so amazed and overwrought that tears fill his eyes. "Yes. Funnel all of Russia on them! They can't survive being engulfed by millions of corpses! Dam up the Volga with Russians, and flood them out!"

"Yes," Polyonov says, "it is apparent that we are drawing the line here. It is also apparent that the Germans feel they must have this mountain of trash. So, it goes on." Polyonov pauses, gazes out over the looming hulls of the gutted and truncated buildings. "Our choice is therefore simple. You know, on our collective farm we slaughtered a lot of pigs, usually in a room about the size of this one." This irrelevance makes Lubko gesture at the ceiling in exasperated appeal. "The pigs would be driven in one by one, and we would put our knives into the jowls and cut their jugulars and send them off to bleed, where they would go on eating and grunting until they died. Well, this one pig apparently knew what was up because when we went after him he became enraged and simply would not let us catch him. All the time he screamed, with what sounded like some strange logical argument carried out at the top of his lungs. In any case, he was so deft, so athletic, that he had the three of us on the defensive for a long time. We finally got him, but the point is that he interrupted our work so much that the other pigs waiting outside got to live an extra day. He was no ordinary pig."

"Well," Lubko says to the wall, "how do you like that? My friend tells me a story about pigs! How interesting!" Then he turns to Polyonov. "Well, how about a story about swans? Or horses? Or ducks? I'd love to hear one about ducks."

Polyonov laughs. "I thought you'd see what I meant. I'm sorry." He pauses, looks out through the window. "Our choice is a simple philosophical one. If we don't attack, we die, all of us. If we attack, a few of us will live, or all of us will die. The only answer is that you have to be brave and go forward. It's very simple, even for a cynic. Bravery is our only chance."

"You mean we might be forced into being heroes of the Soviet Union?" Lubko asks with infuriated contempt.

"Exactly," Polyonov says, "it's all set up that way. You don't think anybody would be stupid enough to give us a choice, do you?"

"Hah! So what are our chances?"

"On the weak side, at best."

"Oh, no," Lubko says, seeing a hunched figure running in the direction of their observation post. "Here comes Comrade Gusev. It's our orders."

"Ah, our orders."

Lubko watches the running figure for a moment, then says, "So what do you suggest we do?" He turns to Polyonov. "Eh? What do we do?"

Polyonov is no longer listening. He crosses himself and whispers into his folded hands.

"I see," Lubko says, sighing. "So that's it, then."

EASTERN POLAND, FALL 1942
Revolt

Ours was a small work camp in which Russians and Poles were kept as a labor force. My function, that of cook for the SS officers, provided me a neutrality that spared me the life of desperation of the average prisoner. Food is a necessity for prisoners, but excellent food is a necessity for the Germans. I cook with the exactitude of a chemist.

The uprising I refer to took place on a Thursday, while I roasted ducks for the officers' dinner. Anatoli Tchilkov, a powerful Russian with a pink, iridescent dueling scar on his face that would have been more appropriate on an aristocratic German, overpowered two guards, who were ordered to execute him into a ditch. Since no one had observed him shooting the guards, he was able to turn back into the camp and attempt a revolt, first ordering a surprised compatriot to study one of the guards' small-bore rifles in order to educate himself as to its use. They were then able to strangle a Ukrainian guard and take his weapon. After this, they lured another prisoner into the guard's outbuilding and easily convinced him to join them, and the three took off their dirty prisoner's smocks and put on the clean, military uniforms. Tchilkov roared with laughter at his having to truss himself up in the largest uniform, so that the cap sat high on his head and his neck veins bulged over the collar, reddening his dueling scar.

They found an SS untersturmführer shaving in the barracks and slit his throat with his razor while he watched with horror in his mirror. Tchilkov cleaned the razor off with a high-command document.

The two other prisoners brought in two frightened officers, who were young and at first assumed that some negotiation was possible. After they were bound and gagged, there ensued a brief orgy of mutilation. Tchilkov and his men then ventured further toward the center of the camp, absorbing into their revolt three more willing prisoners. It was at this point that they entered the kitchen. As I watched, Tchilkov eyed me with curiosity and picked at a nearly done duck he had snatched from the oven, while his men quickly gorged themselves on what was available. Tchilkov muttered contented little grunts of pain from being burned by the duck, apparently still trying to decide what to do with me. Finally he said in fractured Polish I could barely understand, "Good, good, yes. Delicious. Do not talk—you die if you talk." They left me to clean up after them and prepare a new duck for the oven.

Moments later, as I continued my work, I saw, through a window, strange movements of men near the command post, some two hundred meters away. SS soldiers were doing something clearly out of the ordinary. Quickly weighing its meaning, I went to the mess hall phone and informed an unterscharführer as to Tchilkov's activities. By this time, the revolt had advanced; they had managed to recruit two more prisoners who had donned the uniforms of their SS victims. Somewhere near a tool and matériel warehouse, Tchilkov and his men encountered what appeared to be a group of prisoners working in a ditch. But these workers, whom Tchilkov assumed to be candidates for his revolt, turned out to be SS soldiers and Ukrainian guards wearing prisoners' smocks, and the little army was overpowered and confined. My calculations had been correct. In the next few hours, the camp heard the lengthy and careful interrogation, carried out in part with the stolen razor. One could hear the screams from a great distance.

So ended Anatoli Tchilkov's uprising—but another signal of history's bestial symmetry. The investigating officer's behavior toward me hinted at no suspicion, and the same was true of the prisoners in my block. What matter is it, after all, to inform on people who have already failed at their deception? That evening, the sullen and frightened officers were served my dinner, and it seemed to calm them. Later, in the kitchen, as I stripped the remainder of the meat from the ducks, I was complimented by two high-ranking officers, who, as always, showed no mistrust as they looked at me with a knife in my hand.

THE UKRAINE, FALL 1942
A Practical Joke

Dieter Gebhardt was only eighteen, the youngest in our group. He had that thick-lipped, androgynous look about him, with a child's almost hairless face and large, beautiful eyes. His hair was ash blond; had Himmler seen him, he would have instantly become a poster soldier. But he was not a poster soldier; he was a killer of a special kind, puncturing women and children with his PPK, always with a strange smile on his face, along with a look of experimental curiosity, as if he were pulling into himself for the purpose of deliberately savoring the moment.

Some of the older members of our little rural death squad hated him for his beauty and his happy enthusiasm. You must not enjoy this; there was something sick about enjoying this.

At night we were usually drunk, and one night we began to wonder, had Gebhardt ever had a woman? When he came into our quarters, Duerbacher asked him, "Say, Gebhardt, have you ever done it with a woman?"

Gebhardt's beautiful face went into a sneer of disgust.

"Of course not!" he snapped. His voice still had that tendency to trail upwards into falsetto. "It's a waste of time, a lot of stupidity you older men prattle about."

"You're not a man until you've had a woman," Duerbacher said. "Some of these little girls you shoot with your pistol could use a little before they go."

"I would never touch any but an Aryan."

"Come, have a drink with us."

"Drinking is for fools and old men," Gebhardt said.

Duerbacher watched him swagger off and said, "That little pig's ass. Why were we ever saddled with a little bastard like that?"

Duerbacher needled Gebhardt about women every night for a week or so and tried to get him to drink with us. I was against it because his presence would ruin the moody indulgence I had become used to after doing the things I had been ordered to do. But my problem is another story.

One night we managed to get Gebhardt drunk. Through it all, even with his speech slurring, he maintained that youthful insolence that so enraged Duerbacher. But on this night Duerbacher seemed to smile a lot and to indulge the young egomaniac, as if he were one up on him. Finally Duerbacher said, "My boy, I've saved you an Aryan—she's in the back room in the bed, you know, the big room at the end of the hall. We drugged her. She's a virgin, like you, and we thought it would be more humane to knock her out. But if you're going to invade that sacred grotto, son, you'd better do it now. She's the type who would fight, and if she wakes up—"

Gebhardt looked at the hall, then at Duerbacher, blinking slowly, the facade of insolence gone for a moment.

"What is this?" I whispered to Duerbacher. He merely shook his finger in front of my face. I didn't mind because I was drunk.

"Her hair is like spun gold," Duerbacher said. Gebhardt blinked slowly, laboring to focus on him.

I knew something was wrong now because a Ukrainian guard was hanging around, long after he was supposed to have been dismissed. He had a smile like Duerbacher's on his face. "She's in there naked and sleeping," Duerbacher said, "and just bursting with the bloom of youth."

"What is her name?" Gebhardt asked.

"Helena," Duerbacher said. "Pity, she's a partisan."

"Since when do we—" I began, but Duerbacher cut me off and told me to drink my schnapps. Then he said to Gebhardt, "Do you know how to do it, I mean where to—"

"Of course!" Gebhardt said. "Do you think I am stupid? Naturally I shall have to shoot her afterwards."

"Naturally," Duerbacher said, "but hurry up. You'll see, once you give it to her you'll be into all the good-looking ones you find."

"This is contrary to our orders," Gebhardt said.

Duerbacher waved that off with a sneer and said, "Look, the older you get the less in the way of juice you have. This is why you should not be wasting it the way boys your age always do."

"I resent what you imply," Gebhardt said. This seemed to fire the little killer up. He took another long swallow of his drink and marched unsteadily down the hall.

"What's going on here?" I asked Duerbacher. "What's he doing here?" We both looked at the guard, a tall man who snickered at us with a kind of dirty complicity. Then he, too, slipped down the hall.

Duerbacher rose from the table, tested his balance briefly, and said, "It won't work if we take too much time." Then the guard came out from the hallway and nodded.

Duerbacher cleared his throat and called, "Gebhardt, if she seems a bit unresponsive, even cold, it's because she's dead. Check the back of her neck—there's a little hole our Russian friend put there a little while ago."

There was a short silence that was then shattered by a series of shrieks, as if Gebhardt had been scalded. He came running out into the front room holding his pants together at the waist, his face ashen and his body trembling.

"How was she?" Duerbacher asked, then adopted a look of sudden astonishment. "But wait! You've got it backwards! You've deflowered a corpse! It's the other way around!"

The Ukrainian guard burst out into hoarse laughter, and poor Gebhardt bolted from the room.

"That was a horrible thing to do," I said. "A horrible thing. A horrible thing. My God, that was horrible."

Duerbacher looked at me scornfully, thinking. Then he said, "I agree. It most certainly was."

Gebhardt remained the insolent killer, and Duerbacher seemed baffled by this. Apparently he had thought that the experience would make some impression on the young man.

SOEST, GERMANY, FALL 1942

The Dead on the Way to Their Resting Place

The small group, all dressed in black and made up of old men, women, and children, stands before the boxcar, whose open doors reveal a wall of pine caskets stacked on pallets. The people are here to claim the bodies of their sons and husbands. This ritual consists of the solemn acknowledgment of the names of the dead and the silent labor of the station workers, hunched down in the vapor of their breath as they remove the caskets from the car. From the center of the station, the sound of reunions reaches the workers' ears. Then a soft voice: Knappe? Is there a Knappe here? An old woman shuffles forward. A station worker rises, frowning, sniffs the air, and thinks, then returns to his work.

Someone in the back of the group is jostled by an old man with a cane, whose face is lined with anger and sadness. He mumbles under his breath, watching a casket pass him on a four-wheeled cart. The old man pushes forward, his eyes bright with curiosity and indignation. He holds his cane before him, shakes it.

When the last casket for Soest has been removed and placed on a cart before a young woman, the old man with the cane pushes to the front of the group and says in a high, tortured voice, "Gottfried! Gottfried!" The young woman is suddenly ashen and puts herself between the old man and the casket.

"What is this?" she says. "Who are you?"

"Gottfried!" he says, gasping, "Gottfried!"

"You are mistaken," the woman says, her face white, "this is no time for nonsense! This is my husband—he was killed in the East!"

A young woman comes running down the ramp and stops, out of breath. "Grandpa!" she says. "Please!"

"Gottfried!" he says, shaking his cane.

"Please." She goes to him, takes his arm. "Excuse my grandfather," she says to the woman. "I'm sorry. He's a little senile." His eyes blaze. "My father, his son, was killed in Serbia in the Great War—he has never forgotten."

The woman pauses, turning to the casket. "It is nothing," she says. The train hisses and continues on its journey. Silent, the old man watches the cars rumble past. When the train is gone, it reveals a space of tracks and another train that has stopped to take on water. This one is made up of small boxcars with little barred windows, and in each window they see two, sometimes three, pale and unshaven faces with sunken, hopeless eyes, above bone-white hands with almost blue knuckles clutching the bars. As the sound of the other train fades, they begin to hear children crying, men moaning, and, in the wafting of subtly warmer air from the train, there is the stench of sweat and human filth.

"Who are they?" the granddaughter asks.

The old man mumbles, deep in thought. He seems to be trying to remember something.

The woman whose husband lies in the casket looks thoughtfully at the wood. "I wonder if we should open—to identify—"

The station worker who has called the names and helped to unload the boxcar looks across the tracks at the train, which jerks and moves slowly on its way, the pale and emaciated fists still gripping the bars. "It would not be advisable," he says.

NEAR STALINGRAD, WINTER 1943
What Snow Does

The men are grouped out of the wind, protected by their immobilized tank. Only Gerd Bock is active, circling the tank and speculating on how to get it going again. He is a new recruit and has not yet been worn down by the cold. The oil has congealed in the motor; nearby there are trucks, other tanks, and more soldiers hunched around weak fires, waiting for the weather to change. Even the automatics hardly work. Bock stays warm by walking in circles on the brilliant snow that feels packed as hard as stone under his boots. He looks toward the flat plain but can see only ten or fifteen meters because of the snow; this is a good sign, he thinks: snow, precipitation, warmth. The snow swirls softly off the turret and settles in little circular eddies just beyond the meager fire they have kept going with dry-rotted fenceposts.

He returns to the men, who are balled up in their coats, their faces buried inside their collars. Rentzel wears a woman's stole around his neck, an insult to the uniform that makes Bock cringe with embarrassment. "Listen," he says, "we could find a way to use the fire to warm the motor up. Then, if we keep it running—"

"Petrol," Neumann says in a muffled voice, not raising his head.

"It's snowing," Bock says, surprised at their calm lethargy. "This means—"

"Snowing?" Schiel says with exaggerated wonder. "It is? Why, yes, it is *snowing*."

"Be quiet," Neumann says.

"But Bock has told me that it is snowing! I never realized it—look. See how it falls! Why, I've been in Russia in my Sixth Army for months, and yes! I see that it is snowing! Snow! It's white—what a revelation! Say, did you know that snow is white?"

"You didn't let me finish," Bock says.

"Snow is white!" Schiel yells. "The world at large should be informed of this—excuse me for shouting, but information of such importance—"

"You didn't let me finish. I was saying—"

"That snow is white," Schiel whispers with intense, bewildered fascination.

"Shut up!" Neumann snaps.

"I am sorry. I only wanted to share my enthusiasm for—"

"Just stop it," Neumann says.

"I feel a sound," Rentzel says. He raises his face out of the woman's stole.

"What?"

"I feel a sound, in the ground, a rumble."

"Can one feel sound?" Schiel asks with bright curiosity. "This is an interesting if not perversely cryptic phenomenon. Technically, sound waves—"

"I can hear it," Neumann says. He looks around.

The men slowly raise their faces from the collars of their coats and look past the vapor of their breaths at the falling snow. They hear the subtle clinking of metal and feel a strange shudder under them.

"Yes," Bock says. "I feel it now."

Then, in a nightmarish shift, they are suddenly enveloped in the shapes of horses, above which glint the hideous arcs of sabers, and there is the smell of animals and the snorts of breath vapor and after that the flat reports of automatics and bullets plinking off the tank. They are gone as quickly as they have appeared, so that the men around the fire have had time only to slam themselves into the ground. Bock looks after the vanished images of the horses, his mouth full of the taste of metal and his body paralyzed with fright. He tries to speak. The men, save for Rentzel who is still on the ground, have risen to their sitting positions to gape at each other in shock, then at the fire, spitting steam from lumps of snow thrown by the horses' hooves. For Bock, the vision returns slowly: The horses were hairy and black, the uniforms were those of Russians. He even saw the broad, savage faces.

With a quaking voice, he says, "Cavalry. They are using cavalry. We haven't a chance."

Neumann is standing, his automatic out from under his coat. "Cavalry," he says, "of course." Now they see the men from one of the other tanks, moving around with their automatics ready. "They'll be back," Neumann says. "My God, cavalry. Of course. The oil in horses doesn't congeal."

Schiel leans over and puts his hands on Rentzel's shoulder. Rentzel falls back, and his arms flop outward into the snow. The side of his head is split and bleeding, and the vapor from the wound rises into the brittle air like tongues of white fire. "Look," Schiel says.

"He's dead," Neumann says. "There's nothing we can do."

"Godless barbarians," Schiel says. "Look how the blood contrasts against the snow. Poor Rentzel with his lady's stole."

Neumann's face is now flushed with fury. "You will shut your mouth! I promise I'll kill you if you don't shut your mouth."

Schiel looks at him with wan indifference. "Please do," he says. "My hands and feet are cold."

Neumann stomps off toward the other tanks.

"Now," Schiel says to Bock. "Excuse my impertinence before. You've yet to understand what snow does to a person. You were saying about how it is snowing?"

But Bock isn't listening. He is looking at the strange vapor rising from the wound on Rentzel's head.

LENINGRAD, FEBRUARY 1943
Death Visits: An Eyewitness Account

I was perhaps only a kilometer from the river, walking unsteadily along banks of dirty, hardened snow, which months later would melt and reveal the true magnitude of this catastrophe: the frozen dead, sheet-wrapped corpses of the old and the very young. My hunger and fever were such that the snow undulated like windblown wheat, and buildings, lampposts, ice, all mumbled with subtle voices or rattled with an arrhythmic hammering. The ground was not level under my feet. Then a figure blocked my path, that of an ageless, fair-haired man with a handsome but evil face. It was dusk, and when I glanced to my side into the black mirror of a building window I saw that his form made no image there. I was aware of a strange pressure in the air, an uncomfortable density that forced my body to tense with resistance. I heard a soft, exultant laugh. "Do you think you can help anyone now?" The voice was strange and hollow, as if coming from some great distance.

"I comfort the dying. I buoy their faith. It is my duty."

"Whose Russia do you think this is, priest?"

"Politics never compromises faith. Time will prove this."

"Faith—a bit of ass's skin."

A playful expression crossed his malevolent face, and he thought for a moment. "I will show you faith," he said. "Come with me." I followed, my shoes making a brittle, metallic squeaking in the snow. Destroyed buildings swelled and vibrated, and the dissonant hammering echoed from the earth. He led me through a long alleyway past a gutted building where poor flats had been, and then toward the river. I assumed we were somewhere near Nevsky Prospekt but was not sure. The city had been so damaged that I had lost my sense of direction, and the fever further confused me. Finally he stopped at a doorway to a shabby residential building.

He beckoned me to the door. Feeling an increase of that strange pressure, I went in ahead of him, holding my breath at the thought of our closeness at that moment, as if I could breathe in the same air that had come up from the polluted depths of his lungs. But I was not afraid.

Dark as it was in the flat, which was not occupied, I could see across the room the dull golden background of an ikon framed in black wood, which seemed to pulsate like a heart. "Over here," he said. I went to a counter by a broken window, where the light was flat and harsh and charged with vibration. The counter was strewn with rudimentary utensils, pots with cracked handles, crazed dishes, an earthenware crock.

He pointed to a large pot. "Look here," he said. I looked into the vessel: It was empty save for the musty smell of food cooked days or weeks ago. "Look closely." I tipped it toward the window, catching the cold twilight reflected off the snow. The small bits clinging to the inside in the suggestion of a ring three-quarters of the way toward the top and around the bottom were curled fingernails, dry and light, small enough to be those of a child. What I saw had the lucidity and awful stillness of something seen under a powerful microscope. I replaced the pot and went to my knees to pray for the child's soul. He disappeared then, and the pressure I felt relaxed.

I left a few minutes later, pausing to determine where in the city I had been led. I was lost, but I felt relieved when gradually the voices and the hammering from brick and snow and metal and the trickery of the ground under my feet delivered me from the grip of that hideous vision.

WARSAW GHETTO, SPRING 1943
Defense

She had inherited the pistol from her friend Jacek Wyzinski, who was stood against a wall and shot while she watched from the apartment window, holding the gun in her hand. He had spat at them before they did it. Later she heard the sound of heavy boots on the stairs and knew she had no more than a minute or two left. But she was no longer bothered by that; the executions, the bombings, the fires, the constant sound of guns had all achieved a dreamlike familiarity, like getting used to the uneven jerk of a train on a bad track. She did not know why they all had to be executed or taken to the Umschlagplatz for the cattle-car ride to that place of murder that sounded like the tinkling of a bell. But she was not bothered. Almost none of her family was still alive, and the loneliness she felt at being left behind pushed her to the point of being almost eager for release from all this. She was just too tired. All she wanted now was the quick and painless bullet in the head. The alternative, gas, wasn't bad, but she felt a kind of frustrated weariness at the thought of the process, the protracted fatigue of making it, finally, to her own turn, where that one long indrawn breath would do it. So the sound of the boots and the promise of the easier way out made her feel complete and relaxed.

Within a minute she was staring down at the pistol, whose sharp-ended trigger had pierced her index finger. The little blue-edged wound leaked blood, and on the floor before her lay a German soldier. Only then did she realize that, when the figure had blocked out the doorway light, she had pointed the pistol and emptied it at him. Now, her finger still pinned by the sharp lance of the trigger, she saw his form clarifying in her vision like a photograph in a chemical solution.

He had soft blond hair parted in the middle, a ring on one of his right-hand fingers, and nails bitten down to the flesh. She managed to pull her finger off the trigger and put it in her mouth. She was suddenly overcome with a peculiar sensation of terror at the thought of still being alive. She was supposed to make her way to the back of the building, where her uncle was to meet her, but she could not move. She began to cry, could feel each of her organs moving inside her body with nonsensical persistence, in pointless defiance of the obvious. She was a tiny speck of soiled protoplasm sitting on the edge of some welcoming, black abyss, and she did not have the courage to jump.

Movement. The soldier was alive; he seemed to be struggling to turn over, and then he said something with a soft, almost adolescent voice. She held her hands to her face. My God, I've hurt him, I've hurt him. She scrambled to him, almost blinded by her flooding eyes. "Oh, my God," she said, "where are you—" He looked toward her, but his eyes were strange, locked on some semiconscious middle distance. The only blood she could see was in his hair, small flecks of it. "Where are you hurt?" she asked him. He blinked, seemed to be thinking.

"Where are you hurt?"

He muttered something else, sighed, and then his teeth began to chatter. He had tiny white pimples on his chin.

"I'll get my uncle," she said, and ran down the hall. She found him where he had said he would be, at the back of the building. "There's a man—a German soldier—"

"You're late. What did you do to your hand?"

"He's hurt—I—I shot him and he's hurt."

"I've found our way out," her uncle said. "We're leaving."

"Listen, I shot him and he's *hurt*."

"Good for you," he said. "We're going to the forests—wrap up your hand. We're going out with Jewish partisans. You didn't know there were any, did you?"

"But he's no older than I am! My God, we can't—" She broke down again, felt almost breathless. "I shot him, I shot him and he's hurt!" Her finger began to sting, and the pain made her feel suddenly calm. "You mean we're not going to—to Tinkalinka?"

"No, we're not going to Tinkalinka."

She suddenly felt weak. "I'm hungry."

"Good, I've got some bread back at the flat—then we're going under the wall."

"No Tinkalinka?"

"No." He led her down the hall to a steep flight of stairs. "No Tinkalinka. In the cellar we have to be quiet."

She followed her uncle. It struck her that never ever in her life would she be able to erase the blot on her soul for having shot the blond boy, and she knew that there would never be a day when she would not worry about him.

AUSCHWITZ, POLAND, SPRING 1943
The Sonderkommandos' Repast

The four Kapos sit on a bunk, looking down at a grainy chunk of bread the size of a man's hand. It is illuminated by a burning taper held above by Mandel, the "dentist." His job is removing gold fillings and bridges from the mouths of the dead. Dulpers, whose job is furnace tending, prepares to cut the bread five ways using a small gold pocketknife he had pried from the hand of a gassed woman on her way to the oven. Kretchmer and Müller watch, frequently looking over their shoulders toward a nearby bunk where body-carrier Steigl lies. He is the only other Kapo awake in the block. The five men have sacrificed this hour of sleep to divide the bread, which was smuggled in by a Ukrainian guard whom they had bribed with gold fillings and currency stolen from personal effects. A pause in the sure process of their starvation, the bread is even more valuable because the cold weather gnaws at them physically and because the SS have cut their food rations as punishment for damage to a furnace.

The feast of the bread is to be a solemn occasion, for Steigl has told them he cannot eat and will die tonight. He has been here too long and will not make roll call tomorrow. Müller had reported to the others that Steigl had suddenly begun to whisper in his hunger and exhaustion about the past, his family, his native town. "I think it is a bad sign,"

Müller had said, and Kretchmer had replied, "It means he has lost his hold, yes."

Dulpers takes a breath and begins to cut the bread, carefully figuring the first slice at one-fifth. "Five ways," he whispers. "Watch—we'll draw straws to see who chooses first."

The men watch, breaths held. When he is at the point of starting the third cut they all hear noise outside and pause briefly to listen. Guards are beating someone near the transport workers' blocks. "That's way beyond the fence," Kretchmer says. Dulpers nods and continues cutting the bread. When he has finished, the men look at each other with tentative satisfaction. It may mean extra days, maybe weeks of life. The risk is worth it.

Müller rises and tiptoes through the darkness to Steigl's bunk. He leans down to him, saddened by the older man's hairless emaciation, and whispers, "Come, the bread is ready." Steigl opens his eyes, and Müller sees the taper flame reflected in them. "Come," he says, "it's better to eat it sitting up."

Steigl's head moves, just perceptibly. He blinks slowly, then looks at the ceiling.

"No, you're not going up the chimney. We'll work something out, hide you here. We'll organize food."

Steigl's eyes say no. Then, with great effort, he whispers, "Finished."

"No, you only need rest. I will hold the bread for you."

Steigl whispers, "Finished."

He dies while they eat the bread.

Müller discovers this after he has finished his portion, which he has eaten while discussing the possibility of hiding Steigl under a bunk. After all, there are so many men at roll call, some deception could easily be arranged. But Steigl is dead.

Returning to the other men, Müller whispers, "He sleeps with the angels." In the dim light the men study each other's faces, and then they look down. Finally Dulpers sighs and takes out the little knife. "Four ways," he says. Very carefully he measures out the portions while the other men watch.

KHARKOV, THE UKRAINE, SPRING 1943
Infection

Christian Bernsdorf believes he is dying. The long, infected wound on his leg, begun by the shallow slice of a star of barbed wire, is now purplish black, and the inside top of his right leg is knotted with swollen stones of lymph glands, which radiate powerful stabs of pain into his trunk like low-voltage electric shocks. He wavers from fever to cold, from a stinging clarity of vision—the glittering muck of his ditch littered with lumps of equipment and sleeping men—to the soft universe of dreams, where he lives in an infinity of changing settings. There are no medical supplies. The Russians are over there somewhere. The knots of lymph flash pain with the rapid beating of his heart.

A face appears above him: Richter, unshaven, hollow eyed, and no longer looking at Bernsdorf with that wince of vicarious pain. "Do you hear that sound?" he asks.

Bernsdorf thinks. Yes, he feels it in the ground, has for some time, but had confused it with the subtle convulsions of his body. "Those are the Russians," Richter says.

"Yes."

"How do you feel?"

"Fine. I feel fine."

The face disappears. Bernsdorf closes his eyes.

The general gives you a shiny object. You are on the kitchen floor, two years old, fascinated by its brightness. It is the device with which he cleans his smooth, jowled face. You see in his stern but appreciative gaze the truth of your great promise. He holds his uniformed arm out to her. They are going to the cinema. They dissolve through the door, surrounded by white light. Alone on the kitchen floor you open the device and study it. Across the palm of your hand there appears a dotted line of blood connected by a tiny line the thickness of a hair. You laugh, staring at the expanding dots. The device flashes light at you, leaving spots that sweep across the field of your vision. In the far distance you hear the liquid, velvet sound of bugles. You draw the device along your forearm and the release of blood that wets your lap eclipses all doubt, and you find yourself shuddering with a giddy, rubber-legged pleasure. A mystery is solved.

We are counterattacking.

The general melts through the door. He is going to the cinema. Her dress burns with white light at the edges. You look down at the device in—

"Christian."

"What?" Mud, lumps of equipment, the legs of men. Muzzles of rifles. "I can't walk."

"We have orders to counterattack."

"I can't walk. I will stay here."

"We'll come back for you."

"Yes, I'll wait. Be careful."

"Are you cold?"

"No."

"Do you have rations?"

"Yes, I have rations."

The ground rumbles. They are gone to the east. Bernsdorf stares at the mud of the ditch, calculating the speed of his heartbeat. It is as if he had been running. He thinks, the general will explain it, and the pain races through his body. He waits for his entry into the other world. *The general will explain it.*

MAIDANECK, POLAND, SPRING 1943
Moslems

The three inmates stand at the fence, draped in tattered rags and staring at a line of angular, leafless trees in the distance. In camp slang, they are called "Moslems." The two camp guards, usually unaware of those who have lost the will to live and are simply waiting for a comfortable way to die, now watch the three men, wondering what it is that attracts their attention. Reismann, the younger of the two, is fascinated by Moslems because of their closeness to death. The term identifying them seems grimly appropriate: With rags covering their heads, they wander in a catatonic trance, so near to being dead that nothing touches them.

Voss, the second guard, is Reismann's voluntary mentor. He has assisted the younger man in his first month here at the camp by explaining to him the details of its operation and by instructing him in its slang and peculiar social order. "Moslems," he told Reismann, "are retired, no matter what their age is." If, for example, one of those three men at the fence falls down, he will simply curl up into a fetal position and die there, and the other Moslems will not even notice. It is hard to say what degree of awareness they have, but they don't seem to feel pain and are no longer hungry.

"Why don't they just herd them into a gas chamber, then?" Reismann asks.

Voss holds his shoulders up in a sustained shrug.

Reismann watches. The three Moslems stare at the trees. Growing cold and bored, Reismann stamps his feet to get his circulation going again. Then, as he watches, one Moslem gingerly sits down in the mud and slush at the fence. "Look," Reismann says to Voss.

"Yes, he's gone. He'll be there tomorrow, ice cold."

Reismann watches. The two Moslems still standing shuffle a short distance away, as if giving the third the proper space to die. Reismann leans his rifle against the wall, steps out of the guard shack, and walks toward the Moslems. "Don't touch them!" Voss calls after him. "Typhus!"

Reismann approaches the Moslems. The one who had sat down is now balled up, his face nestled in the dirty slush; he stares at the mud just in front of his face. Reismann gains the attention of one of the other two, an old man perhaps in his sixties whose watery, red-rimmed eyes set in the stubbly, emaciated face rest on him with casual objectivity. "What are you looking at?" Reismann asks. "What do you see out there?" The Moslem seems to think, weighing Reismann's question as if it is almost mystifyingly complicated.

"Trees," he whispers.

"Why? What's so interesting about trees?"

The Moslem looks at the trees. "A swan."

"Swan? What swan?"

"In the trees," the Moslem whispers.

Reismann looks, baffled. "One, two, three," the Moslem whispers. "There—see?"

Reismann grunts and leaves the men. In the shack he says to Voss, "Insane. They are insane."

Later, near sundown, Reismann watches the western sky go from yellow to orange and feels the chill advance. The two Moslems are gone; the third remains sleeping in the mud and slush. It is only a few minutes before the changing of the guard. Reismann sighs and looks at the color in the sky above the line of trees. Then, in a peculiar transformation of his vision, he sees a shape that, in a matter of seconds, materializes into the Moslem's swan, sitting facing south with its long, graceful neck lined with an artist's perfection by the limbs of two trees meshing with one another. Even the wing tips rising slightly off its back are included in the picture, and the soft, rounded beak sits exactly where it should be, as if the two trees had been bent together with an almost agonizing precision. He steps out of the shack and walks to his left, to some higher ground where he can get a better look, but, as he moves laterally, the swan disappears as magically as it had appeared. One had to stand exactly where the Moslems had stood in order to see it.

EASTERN POLAND, SPRING 1943

Blessed Mongrel

What bothers Gran now, silent and thoughtful as we walk on through the woods, is the corpse. Of course we had seen others, snow caking their eyes and the corners of their mouths, lying next to burned-out trucks and wagons. Gran would tell me not to breathe near them, and we would walk on. But this corpse was different. He was a partisan whose forearms were frozen in the position of moving to clasp his hands in prayer; a small dog chewed at his face, shivering and looking with sheepish fright at us. The man lay on his back on a round patch of icy crust, and midway down his body there seemed to be a pivot, so that the little dog moved him easily as if he were a two-pointed dial. When the dog pulled at his lip, he pointed one way; when he let go, the partisan slid slowly back and pointed another way, moving nearly a quarter turn. "Hold your breath!" Gran hissed, when she understood what she saw. "Be careful now, hold your breath!" We hurried past. A little farther away Gran took out her icon and set it up on a tree stump. It has a pinched and thoughtful-looking Madonna cradling a doubtful little Jesus. Gran prayed to it and waited for a message, but she gave up when her knees became cold on the hard snow, and we packed up and moved on.

Still we walk through the forest, Gran in her rumpled clothes with the bag slung over her shoulder and her walking stick in her hand, and I wearing three layers of clothes, making me feel as if I am tied inside a wad of hay. Gran is still trying to figure out the strange message of the partisan. She mumbles from an almost toothless mouth, fingers a mole on her chin, her eyes distant and afraid. At times we stop so that she can sprinkle ancient herbs on the snow, trying to read them, muttering to herself. This scares me because she usually scoffs at the supposed value of herbs, says that those with true vision don't need them. Then she uses her secret language, which she has said can be uttered for good use only twenty times in a life; she is on her knees again, and it sounds like, "Draxy draxy steepstichen!" She looks up, sighs miserably, and struggles back to her feet.

"What does that mean?" I ask.

And she says, "It means too much to translate—a thousand normal words or more. I could never explain it." Then she cuffs me on the head. "What would a ten-year-old mongrel know, anyway?"

We walk on.

We are going to Dnisy to escape the Germans. She calls me her blessed mongrel, half Jew and half Pole, and has told me that the spirits have instructed her that I must be saved because pure blood is a curse. "Everybody hates everybody," she told me, thinking deeply as she talked, tapping the one yellow tooth in the front of her mouth with her nail. "The Germans and Bolsheviks will cancel each other out. The meaning of your blood is that, if you marry, say, a Ukrainian girl and your son a Finn and so on for a hundred years, eventually the only way to make war will be to slit one's own throat." When she dressed me, she told me not to be afraid because she had cast around herself an electrical shield, a globe of protection. Then she made me walk past her so as to feel it. I did—it felt like a combination of heat and the opposite of magnetism.

The day is waning, and Gran's preoccupation with the partisan makes her look older; she walks stooped over, listening intently to her inner voices. Through the trees we can see columns of black smoke in the distance. Gran stops again, wearily opens her bag, takes out a little drawstring pouch of some herb and sprinkles a pinch on the snow. She studies the dusted pattern, scratches her chin, running her fingernails on either side of the mole. She waits, looking distant, and I begin to feel cold from lack of movement. Suddenly she grips my wrist with such force that it hurts. "I was right. Dnisy is in ruins and everybody is gone. The partisans are our friends, even yours." Then she whispers something like, "Draxlishnim," and something else I cannot hear. When she is finished, she listens to the wind in the trees, then points her walking stick to our right. "It was obvious from the beginning, but I was afraid we were being deceived by evil forces. The dog *was* a messenger from God. We will find safety this way."

We walk on, and Gran is now very pleased with herself.

AUSCHWITZ, POLAND, SUMMER 1943

Transport Number 420

"No," the boy says, "big people will always give us water. You'll see."

"What's inside there? Why are we all—" his sister's voice softens with doubt. "Will the Night Man—"

"No, that's just something Grandfather made up," the boy says, sighing with fatigue. "There is no such thing." It amazes him that, with all this, she cannot forget a stupid fantasy invented by an old man. Her hand is soft and slick with sweat in his own. They are crowded in among naked men and women, all twice their height. The girl stares with grim fascination at the hairy buttocks of the men and the sagging flesh of the old women, all made more interesting because of the closeness, so that they see it in bizarre, intensified detail—pale flesh and, below, bony ankles and angular, veined feet on the tile floor.

The boy swoons with fatigue and yawns through his burning thirst. Two days. First it was the train, where they were separated from their father. During the ride, where they were crushed in among the big people, they exhausted themselves speculating on where he would be, how they would find him when the ride was over. An old lady even died right in their car. The air was so hot and foul that they could hardly breathe, until the boy discovered a lightless fissure between two boards in the wall, through which he slid the tongue of his shoe, so that they could scoop the fresh air into the car and trade off breathing it. Since his sister was only three, the boy worried about whether or not she got enough, and he gave her more than he took. They would get the good air and hold it in their lungs, which made them dizzy and silly, holding it with puffed cheeks until they exploded with giddy laughter. This worked for almost a day, until a man felt the air on his hand and pushed them away from the hole and took it for himself.

They saw their father on the long platform, but only for a minute and too far away to speak to. They inched in a huge line toward a gate, and all stopped at a uniformed soldier who told them to go either this way, or that. The soldier was very friendly and had a gap between his two front teeth that made his speech whistle slightly. Their father went up the platform, and the boy and his sister through a gate.

The girl begins to cry once more, but weakly, because she has been crying for days; she quickly becomes tired of it and stops. "I'm thirsty," she says.

"They'll give us water soon. You'll see. This place is big; maybe they'll let us play soccer here."

"Can the Night Man—"

The boy looks up and sighs. "No," he moans softly.

The crowd inches forward again. The boy can hear the Germans around the edges telling everyone to go this way, to hurry, there will be soup on the other side. Although there are protests, mostly from angry-sounding men, the crowd moves, the flesh bouncing and jiggling.

They step into another room through a door that has a black rubber edge. In here it smells strange. The girl begins to cry again, and the boy squeezes her hand and says, "Shh, don't worry. Maybe they'll have the water here. Or soup."

"It smells like—like—"

"Shh, shh." Some of the men at the edge of the tightly packed crowd are becoming angry again, but the boy cannot hear what they are saying because of the shuffle of people around him.

They find a little space near a corner, and the girl pushes up against him, her eyes bleary and her face streaked with dirt. Although it embarrasses him, the boy holds her to his side. Then, from above, they hear a sound, like garbage can covers being rattled, followed by the sound of something like marbles, or pebbles, falling to the floor. The boy sees, down among the ankles, a blue-green pebble and suddenly feels a powerful crush accompanied by deafening screaming. His sister's hand is ripped from his, and he is thrown back against the wall, so that his head hits it with a sickening, silver flash. Then it is dark. He reaches for her, but the sound is so loud, the pressure of thighs and hips against him so great that he feels it is suddenly a dream, the deafening sound a peculiar silence, the darkness a strange and ugly light, and the ferocious burning in his throat a fetid and magnetic sweetness. He holds his breath.

CELLE, GERMANY, SUMMER 1943
A Leave

"I'm sorry," she says, "he's just not himself since—"

"Don't think about it," her father says. He understands. He was in the Great War and knows the pressures men must endure and what it is that they cannot say to their families. He glances down the long street, past the ancient buildings with the rectangles of soft orange light in the windows.

"Perhaps tomorrow we'll have a nice time down at the pond. The children love the swans." Her mother nods once, slowly.

"Of course," the father says. He looks at his wife, who now stares back into the darkness of her daughter's house with sympathy and curiosity. "Please explain to Stephan that we understand."

"I will."

After they leave, she returns to the parlor. Stephan sits on the couch wearing his dress uniform with the stiff collar, a drink in one hand and a cigarette in the other.

"Another drink?" she says. "But you got so drunk! You said things nobody understood!"

"I am sorry."

"It's so embarrassing," she says. "What must they think?"

"It won't happen again. What did I say that was so strange?"

"I can't remember. Gibberish. Strange enough that I can't even remember. Stephan—"

"I won't do it again."

"I'm not mad," she says quickly, "nor is Father. He said that in the Great War he had difficulty, too."

"The Great War," Stephan says. "Yes, I suppose he would know."

"It's late. You need sleep."

"I won't be sleeping tonight," Stephan says thoughtfully, "because I am going to drink. I *must* do it, do you understand? I should jot down a few notes. Say, one long swallow every half hour? But then, these measurements might—"

She begins to cry, staring at him.

"Precision," he says, and slumps with fatigue.

"Why are you doing this? What happened in Poland that—"

"Poland? No, what happened, happened only a few minutes ago, in the children's room." He looks at their door. "I was in the room. They are so beautiful when they sleep. Look at how small their wrists are! I realized that I would die for them both if I had to. Eagerly." He pauses. "I had the ashtray in one hand, a cigarette in the other. I realized also that I could kill both of them. The ashtray is heavy, a kilogram at least. I could flatten her skull with it. Then there was the cigarette. I realized that I could put it out on her eye."

She is crying again, harder than before.

"Then I would kill her with the ashtray," he says. "I almost did it. You know that feeling you have just as you jump, say, off a diving board? That sensation of being committed to the air? Well, I felt that, committed to the air. I almost raised the ashtray to cave in her skull." He pauses. "I even saw the ashtray covered with splintered bone, bits of hair, yellowish brain. It does look yellowish sometimes, you know? However, sometimes it doesn't. Peculiar."

"Why? Why do you think these things?"

"These are elemental thoughts."

"Please come to bed."

"Perhaps the one elemental understanding of all," he says softly, "but I must get to my drinking."

He seems suddenly on the edge of sleep. She rises from her chair and removes the cigarette from his limp fingers, the little glass from his hand, and stares, trembling, at the orange tip of the cigarette.

WESTERN RUSSIA, SUMMER 1943
Himmelfahrtskommando

Both Helmut and I had known Brunner from before the war. Once, when we had visited his house near Garmisch, we had run over a chicken in his driveway, and his father had stood there angrily regarding it. I had apologized, but Brunner had cut me off, saying that his father did not own so flat a chicken. The old man's look of stern disapproval had melted from his face. Brunner was a gifted athlete, well bred and good humored, holder of the Knight's Cross. When we saw him off in the distance, working in the hole in the shimmering heat, and then blinked as he went up in the explosion, we looked at each other and then at Sielmann, who smoked one of his French cigarettes and showed no emotion at Brunner's passing. Both of us were close at that moment to admitting what we could do if we had the chance. But we had to move further across the green and amber countryside to clear more mine fields. The shock troops were ahead, the heavy equipment behind. We were not told if we advanced or retreated, but the position of the setting sun told us it was the latter.

In a wood we find a dead partisan, whose body is still warm and whose rifle lies by his side. I am suddenly reminded of what I found left of Brunner a kilometer behind us: boots still containing truncated legs, the lower jaw off his skull. I do not speak to Helmut, but I know his thoughts coincide with mine; they have ever since the three of us heard that BBC broadcast, which landed us, for punishment, in this battalion whose casualty rate is 70 percent. Brunner had laughed at the thought of our title, Himmelfahrtskommando, the brigade bound for heaven. Sielmann, our officer, is a hard Nazi, and we work, toying with our deaths, with the aroma of those cigarettes sometimes wafting across our sweat-slicked faces.

Sielmann is in the half-track, peering over the windshield at us. His driver is gone, wounded by mine fragments and behind the line of advance. In his right hand Sielmann holds field glasses. When he pulls up to ask why we pause by the tree, I indicate the body of the partisan. Sielmann comments on the raggedness of his dress, says that if this is what the Polish-Russian underground amounts to, then why does anyone ever mention it? By this time I am around behind the half-track, putting on my gloves. Sielmann laughs, reaches into his tunic for his cigarettes. I make little noise as I pull the rifle from the bush and aim quickly at the base of his neck and fire. Sielmann lies prone on the hood of the half-track, the blood from the exit wound running off over the right headlight, which is slitted for night camouflage.

I replace my gloves in my pack and return the rifle to the partisan's side. Helmut sits with his head in his hands, asking why so much could go wrong in such a short time. I ask him to remember Brunner and those days before the war, picture Brunner's face, feel his presence. The fact of his death ought to explain it all.

Helmut feels better. In front of the half-track I find Sielmann's cigarettes and we smoke, waiting for the soldiers to arrive later today so that we may explain the tragic nature of Sielmann's death, and perhaps comment on the irony of the raggedness of the culprit's dress.

TREBLINKA, EASTERN POLAND, SUMMER 1943
Horror Stories

Jan Kratko and Anton Zydovska have worked this detail for two days and are finally over the shock of discovering that this remote section of the camp is laid out in large burial pits in the yellow, sandy earth. They speak in low tones whenever the German guard walks away, upwind of the tangy smell of death. The nude bodies arrive in a metal dump cart on narrow-gauge rails, some old and emaciated, some young and healthy, and they must drag them into the pit and arrange them in rows, six tiers deep. They rest before the cart arrives again, standing at the edge of the pit and getting their breath from the heavy work, grimacing from the acidic pain of hunger.

"Chelmno," Zydovska says. "There an officer used to hang men close to the ground and force them to look into his eyes—then he would laugh very loud like a madman."

"Yes, these little jokes," Kratko says. "I have heard of this. At Maidaneck they would lecture to us, always about what low beasts in human form we were, about how all this is nature's way," and he sweeps his hand out over the pit. "Then they'd take a man and boil his hand in a pot until his skin slid off like a glove."

The cart arrives, pushed by two sullen Kapos who tip it up so that the bodies flop out in a limp and angular little avalanche. Then they turn and push the cart back toward the large brick building where the people are killed. On top of the pile of bodies is a young girl different from the others in this group, all of whom are old and thin and dark haired. Although her hair has been cut short, the two men can see that it is the color of wheat, and she is plump and buxom and has a chubby, angelic face. Mildly stunned, Kratko looks away from her face, bothered by the eyes, one of which is open wide, with a pale blue iris, while the other is half shut. On the other side of the pit, the German guard smokes and looks toward the distant pines. Kratko becomes locked in a weary, catatonic sadness, a hollow swoon of memory. Such beauty, he thinks. He reaches out and places his hand on the girl's full breast, and the pressure of the hand makes a soft hiss of air escape from her mouth. "It is a shame," he says.

"Don't do that!" Zydovska whispers harshly.

"It is a shame."

"Don't. Don't!"

Soon she is made anonymous in the sea of flesh. Across the pit, smoke curls away from the guard's head. Struggling for balance on the flesh, Kratko and Zydovska carry the last body, an old woman with a wart on her cheek, and set her out in her final resting place. Returning to the edge of the pit, staggering with exhaustion and aching with hunger, Kratko barely notices that they walk on the girl's back.

Resting, they wait for the cart. "Here," Zydovska says, "there is supposed to be an officer who shoots children for fun. From his porch. A guard throws the child in the air and—" Kratko nods, understanding. "He has a little daughter who watches, too," Zydovska says. "It is said that she enjoys it very much."

Seeing the dump cart approaching, feet and heads rocking at the rim, Kratko grimaces at the thought. "It is not a thing to let children see," he says.

SOBIBOR, POLAND, SUMMER 1943
The Ornithologist

The suicide of Gerd Von Eppen was a shock to the high command. I think of a photograph of him at Sobibor, overseeing a grotesque execution of his own devising. The inmate is being drawn on a small cart by two Kapos crawling on all fours. Von Eppen watches; you can see the pale bags under his eyes and the patches of darker skin below, the delicate web of blasted veins on his cheeks and nose. It is the face of a heavy drinker, but his expression is that characteristic smirk of remorseless humor and vigorous conviction. You will see this in most pictures of us. Perhaps my sensitivity to facial expressions in photographs is due to my previous profession, that of portrait photographer; once I joined the service and the war started, however, I stopped using my cameras and have not touched them since.

In any case, the hanging was done upside down using a scaffold and pulley attached to the inmate's feet, so that, in drawing him up, the strangulation was achieved by a rope attached to the root of a dead tree. The inmate was a baker whose bread Von Eppen had tasted and rejected as inedible, at which he had ordered the baker executed. Bakers, he said with jovial authority, had best learn to bake. Von Eppen was impressive to all of us because of his diabolical inventiveness and his absolute lack of conscience. He was gifted, stately, and educated.

But then, his curious demise, the apparent source of which I witnessed: A group of us were standing near the crematorium, idly talking, uncomfortable in the heat—our uniforms are black and close fitting, and absorb sunlight. Across the barren space of earth between the crematorium and warehouses, groups of prisoners lugged piles of clothing and personal effects from the changing room to the sorting area. Beyond them, a work gang labored in a ditch watched over by guards with whips and rifles. Next to the barracks building lay the corpses of five Kapos, possibly typhus victims. For this reason, we did not go near the barracks.

In one of those hot, sleepy lulls in the general activity, a shape dropped from the sky, light brown and fluid, and landed in the dust. It was a large bird with long blue legs and a thin, downward-curving beak about ten centimeters long. The inmates, noticing that the guards were captivated by the bird, stopped their exhausted shuffling to look. It was a beautiful bird with a round, speckled head and somewhat large, intelligent eyes. Birds usually avoid the camp—the smell probably—and for this reason we were all unable to take our eyes off it. Jerking its head around, it seemed to regard each one of us briefly but individually.

Apparently out of force of habit, one of the guards raised his Mauser to shoot the bird. I waved quickly at him, whispered, "No!" The bird looked at me, took two steps on its blue, delicate legs. "A camera," I said to a colleague. "I want my Leica." But then I flushed with a peculiar embarrassment. It was useless; it had been packed away, and I hadn't had film in years.

Across the space, inmates began to walk again, guards cleared their throats and gave orders. I turned. Von Eppen came toward us with his purposeful stride, lightly rapping his truncheon on his thigh. Who would die today? What error would which inmate commit that would mean his bizarre execution? The prisoners moved as far away from him as possible, making believe they were unaware of his presence. His face had that familiar devastated look, meaning that he had had a bad night.

"Over here," I whispered to him as he approached. "It's a bird. Have you ever seen one like that?"

Von Eppen stopped, looked, then underwent the same moment of adjustment that the rest of us had. Suddenly, his expression changed, and he began looking at the bird with apparent concern, or perhaps with dawning rage. "But—"

"What is it, sir? Is something—"

"A curlew," he said, looking around quickly, sweat beading his face. Now he looked frightened by something, an uncharacteristic expression for him.

"Is it the heat?" I asked.

"*Numenius tenuirostris*," he said, and glanced at his truncheon. "But—" Now he seemed to have lost all color in his face.

"Come out of the sun," I said.

"Probably from the Pripet marshes," he said, "but—" He was now badly shaken and seemed to have trouble keeping his balance. "It cannot see this," he whispered intensely.

"Please?"

"It cannot see this! It cannot see this!" Von Eppen leaned against the building for support. "It cannot!" As if the bird understood, it suddenly took flight, making a sound: "Keewee!"

"Oh, my God!" Von Eppen said. "Oh, my God, it must not see!"

I turned to a guard. "Obersturmführer Von Eppen is ill, help me."

It seems that Von Eppen had studied ornithology before the war. Two weeks after this incident, he was found dead in his office, having shot himself through the heart with a parabellum pistol.

KURSK, RUSSIA, SUMMER 1943
The Musical Prodigy

Budenkov had made up his mind and walked away from the war. The absurd din of artillery, of tank and Katiusha rocket fire, and the ear-shattering buzz of the Stormoviks, all because of him, were too comically exaggerated a development. He took a heavy Degtyarev automatic, carrying it on his back so that the round cartridge pan banged his shoulder with every step. The line he made as he walked was absolutely straight, in watchful disregard for geography. This took him half a day. He hid in a burned-out barn, down in the dark, cool manger, the Degtyarev set up and pointing at a block of doorway light. His fingers were bruised and sore, and he wondered if the little injuries would in any way affect his playing. But the days of music seemed long gone. Briefly he saw himself at ten, playing before the audiences in Odessa and at the spas on the Black Sea. Fifteen years. A century.

He waited. It made no difference who blocked the light, German, Russian, partisan, Kalmuk. The recognition of his secret reality made them all his executioners. He was awakened to this reality upon emerging from a brilliant shellburst, blinking and numb and nearly deaf but otherwise unhurt. Life until then had been like a child's optical illusion on paper—what you are convinced is an urn in silhouette becomes forever two faces nose to nose. Since he was born, the world had lived in perpetual, rigid dread at his very existence, and this war was a collective strategy to corner him unaware and kill him, thus releasing the world into a monumental sigh of relief. He should have known this long ago, when his parents, grooming him for his performances, had treated him like a deadly snake. And now even matter conspired against him; he knew its trickery, the hidden strands of barbed wire on the ground, "stray" bullets, storms with badly aimed lightning bolts. Would his organs, sliding over each other inside that symmetrical arrangement of bones, be the next to mount a conspiracy against him?

He sighed with a sensation of prehistoric fatigue. The sound of the battle, like distant thunder, continued, and he laughed until tears filled his eyes. What idiots! They still didn't know he had left, and so continued their imbecilic charade.

He had a little cheese in his sack but knew food was unnecessary, a stupid human weakness he had assumed applied to him. Still, imagining that he was human was a habit and not unpleasant. He reached for the sack and saw movement in the darker corner of the barn. Groaning with jovial contempt, he turned the Degtyarev and aimed. It was a cat, orange striped. Budenkov stood up straight. The cat came out with an E-sharp "Br-r-raalp?" and slid along the wall toward a beam, seductively arching its back.

"Who sent you?" Budenkov demanded. The cat pointed its rear end to the beam and sprayed, his tail vibrating in a long, vigorous strain. Budenkov sighed. He felt like giving up, letting them do with him whatever they deemed appropriate. He felt like a densely pressurized container of poison of infinite toxicity, and even the cat, circling him along the wall, could not hide his collusion. "I have decided to go to Odessa," he said. He pulled the cheese out of the sack and broke off several crumbs. He threw one to the cat, who ate it quickly, as if fearing its magical disappearance. The cat then approached him. "Very well," Budenkov said, "we shall establish a pact of interim noblesse oblige." He gave the cat another crumb of cheese, and then it understood and allowed itself to be stroked. "Yes, we shall go and let them carry on. They are unaware of my absence! Hear that? All because of someone who isn't even there! Come, we will go to Odessa, and it's a long way."

Budenkov considered taking the Degtyarev but realized he didn't need it. Why participate in their games? He gave the cat more cheese, and they left for Odessa, the cat following him by darting quickly and warily from bush to bush. Walking with that exhilarating sensation that always comes from knowing you are going south, Budenkov noted with interest and curiosity that bombed-out trucks, shattered trees, and obscure lumps of rubble on the ground all sat in careful but oddly benign observation of their passing.

KIEV, FALL 1943
Perpetual Motion

The boy sits on a little stool and watches his grandfather oil the motion device. The old man wants it kept secret, and these last few weeks the boy has wanted nothing more than to tell people about it. Above them the rumble of heavy equipment moving down the street sends fine grit from the basement ceiling, making the old man gaze upward with an expression of beseeching rage, as if the Germans' activity outside is no more than fate playing an annoying joke on him. "Confound it!" he roars, "how in the name of Almighty God—" Then there is a period of silence. The boy can hear the faint tat-tat of machine guns, of people being killed in the ravine. The old man listens, too, looking distant and thoughtful. "Yes," he whispers, "General Zhukov is on the way—and after that, General Winter." He snatches a gray rag off the bench and carefully rubs the strange, gleaming track of the device, which forms a huge circle on a series of roller-coasterlike humps formed by highly polished wood that gleams with a dark brilliance. "One oppressor or another," he mutters, "it's all nonsense."

"How long is a hundred years?" the boy asks.

"I am seventy-five," the old man says. "You are eight. When I set this going, the ball will roll until long after I am gone to argue with my Creator. After you, too."

"What will you say to Him?"

The basement floor shudders with a sustained rhythm, shaking the tall clock device attached to the track. The old man throws his arms around it, looking up. "You lump of dung!" he yells. The boy blushes. "Why do you punish us like this?" Then the rumble stops. "Ah, He has been misled by some Beelzebub, some lord of dog vomit disguised as an advisor. How else could we have commissars, Germans, the Babi Yar ravine?" The old man looks at the gears and pulleys inside the old clock. Then he says, "They shoot people there. Didn't you know that?"

The boy shrugs, then says, "The ball will still be rolling when I am dead, too?"

The old man looks at him questioningly. "Well, yes," he says. "I need only to complete the weight mechanism. It's very complicated."

"Can we put the ball on now?"

"Yes." The ball is a bright silver color. "This is chromium. It cannot rust, or pit. Here, feel its weight." He places the ball in the oily rag and hands it to the boy. "Don't drop it," he whispers. It is like a heavy Christmas ornament. He gives it back to the old man, who places it on the track and then gently sets it in motion. It starts slowly, gains speed, then shoots up one of the many steep slopes on the track, nearly stops, and gains speed again on the gentle incline. When it has made the entire circle, it returns to the clock, and at the top of the steep part of the track, a little arm made from a felt piano hammer snaps out of the clock with a soft click and pushes it on its way.

The old man watches, scratching his chin. "Well, perhaps less than a hundred years—who knows? But there will be thirty kilograms of weight in the pulley mechanism. We shall see."

Later the boy leaves his grandfather, and, a little groggy from watching the ball roll silently on the track, he walks back to his house, hearing again the distant rattling of the machine guns in the ravine. There is supper with his parents, his father's excited speculation about Zhukov, and then dusk. The boy resists the temptation to tell his parents about the motion device. When he goes to bed, everything he thinks of seems superimposed over the tattoo on his mind's eye—the vision of that ball rolling on its track. Nothing in his experience is more amazing than the idea that, hidden in the dusty cellar, the bright ball will still circle the track long after he has grown old and died.

AUSCHWITZ, POLAND, FALL 1943
Children of Wing 22

The children do not know what book it is that Andreas Larkos reads. He is close to no one because he does not speak their language and because one side of his face is marked by a large blotch the color of wine. In their segregated groups of ten or twelve, each tied together by common language or dialect, they speculate that the book, either found in the stone quarry or smuggled into the camp, is on some religious subject. There is no time to ask him about it, using either sign language or the halting German a few of them know from school. In the early morning, when dusty shafts of light come through the little windows and travel up the tiers of dirty bunks, he sits tipping it into the sun, whispering to himself. When the block manageress comes in and whacks her truncheon on the wall, he quickly puts the book out of sight and unconsciously covers the blemish with his hand. The manageress herds the children without food or water out to the quarry to gather small stones all day, each of them moaning with hunger and thirst. The weaker ones, swollen in the legs and sleepy, wilt over the stones and cannot get up. They are carted away, a few each afternoon.

Deep in the night, the children are marched back to Wing 22 and fed a watery soup made with sawdust and potato peelings. Then they immediately crawl into their bunks. Sleep comes quickly.

No one is awakened by the moans or crying of tomorrow's dead.

Andreas Larkos wakes up. When he sits up on the edge of his bunk, an acid stab of hunger thrusts upward into his chest. He rubs the sleep from his eyes and looks around, then reaches under his mattress for the book, feeling among pebbles, snips of paper. It is about science, the universe, the history of beings on earth. Today, on page thirty-seven, he reads about the linear magnitude of time, that the earth is billions of years old, and that it takes a thousand times a thousand to make a million and another thousand times that to gauge half the life of the planet. In his half sleep, he labors over the comparison: *I am nine, man is a thousand times a hundred, a speck in a billion—father was four times my nine when . . .* And he sees him again, how strange the way the wind ruffled his black hair, which usually bore the impression made by his tight hat, and his cheeks so strangely puffed, and the rope gone in the flesh under his jaw.

In the quarry, a boy ahead of him drops on the stones and seems to study the ground close to him with patient, glassy eyes. Then a string of brown bile comes from the corner of his mouth. Andreas puts his hand on the blemish and turns from him to his own shadow . . . *made by the sun, and there are stars a million times bigger, we see only as tiny points of light in the night sky, a million times the size of the sun.*

As he stands on his shadow at midday and fatigue threatens to overcome him, he finds a flat, gray pebble with the imprint of a fossil shell in it, delicate rills fanning outward from the squared base. His heart thumps with excitement at this discovery. It is one of the best he has seen. He has no pockets, so he places the stone in his mouth for safekeeping, to add to the little collection he keeps next to the book under his mattress.

NEAR MOSCOW, WINTER 1944
"Then Time Slowed . . ."

"And so Pashkov rose and said to us, 'The Germans are butchers of children. You will see how Mitka Pashkov treats the butchers of children.' It had been only hours since the poor fellow had learned the news about his family. He picked up his automatic and left." In the firelight, Korilov's thick eyebrows cast heavy shadows upward on his forehead. It was nearly dawn, and soon the men would rise to engage the Germans again. Kliment Tolev felt a dizziness leak through his body; his influenza made his head reel, and his fever numbed the poisonous fear that had burdened him for weeks. A short distance away rose the hulking shapes of destroyed German tanks, yesterday's victory, and now the snow had covered the frozen bodies and the shattered equipment left behind.

"Tolev," Korilov said, "you are only a boy and cannot know the rage one feels at the loss of one's children."

"I understand," Tolev said with a trembling sigh. "Please, go on. I'll find it easy to identify with my father when, I mean, if I'm killed." The men looked at each other, and Korilov nodded his head slowly.

"Pashkov advanced upright toward the German positions," he went on. "I tell you this is true. Five or six of us saw this and confirmed it each to the other." The men leaned toward the fire, interested. "The battle was ferocious—bullets flew above our heads—but Pashkov seemed not to be hit, far ahead of us as he was. He would be gone in the smoke, and then we'd see him again, the automatic at his side, firing at the Germans." Korilov paused, amazed at what he was about to say. "The bullets were ripping through his body—we could see his very flesh being left in chunks behind him on the snow, but he fought on, frightening many Germans into a retreat and killing those who thought he could be stopped." Korilov moved the end of a branch into the embers, shaking his head. "At the end of this engagement, someone brought out vodka and he drank, and then did that same vodka leak like pure water from his bloody wounds. There were no eyes in the sockets of his head, only little blue flames, and he picked up his automatic and advanced again, raising us from our exhaustion to follow him."

"Was he killed?" Tolev asked. "I mean, how could a man—"

"I was coming to that. It was as if this one man, who had lost his children to the butchers, were responsible for a general rout. Listen, we are practical men and could easily discount this as nonsense, but for the fact that we *saw* it. He marched—it was smoky and loud, and then, all of a sudden, time slowed. We could see the very bullets soaring through the air, we could see Pashkov standing there being virtually disemboweled in slowed-down motion, so that organs and strips of flesh flew out behind him, so that chunks of bone and hair from his head flipped back at us. But he advanced onward, right into the front door of a building, killing all who faced him. Later, when we had secured our new position, we looked for him there, but he had vanished without a trace. All we could find were small organs and bits of frozen flesh, scraps of his uniform, a couple of teeth." Korilov leaned back. "It is believed that he still exists, however, because we could not find his gun. He is with us, out there somewhere."

Dawn. Korilov sighed and looked at the men, who studied the embers in the dying fire. There were a couple of glances of fatigued skepticism, a thoughtful cough.

"How many children did he lose?" Tolev asked.

"Two, but one cannot put a figure on that. His vengeance is great."

Tolev rose unsteadily and wandered off toward the German tanks. He had to urinate and decided to do something he had seen other men do, urinate on the corpse of a butcher of children.

Alone among the tanks and bodies, Tolev felt a slimy chill run through him. Because of his fatigue, he went on with his original plan, although the idea now seemed strange to him. He urinated on the snow-covered shape of one of the corpses. As he did so, the snow melted, revealing to him a partly open hand, with two fingers pointing in a westward direction. He finished, staring at the hand, and was suddenly frightened, as if the stream of urine had for a moment been a kind of conduit of death, something like an electrical wire with current in it; then he turned and went back toward the fire, understanding that he had made a fatal error, that now he would almost certainly be killed unless some secret and providential condition could help him past this accidental blasphemy. No, that was it, death had run upstream into his body, and he carried it in his stomach. He shuddered miserably; he felt lonely and deeply afraid, and suddenly very tiny and insignificant in the huge silence. All that told him that he was still alive was his discomfort and the sight of the fire the men were building for breakfast. With that, another idea came to him, that there was always the possibility that he might be protected by that riddled man who had lost his children.

INSIDE WESTERN RUSSIA, WINTER 1944
Lebensraum

Haas, our officer, believed that we were near the border of Poland, and with renewed hope the three of us trudged on, so that little explosions of snow came off our knees. The brightness drove our eyes nearly shut; we saw the endless flat expanse of western Russia only through blazing slits of vision. We had marched for two days and had seen little, until we approached a rise speckled with the black forms of tree stumps. Five kilometers ahead, across snow lifted by the wind like steam off the glittering surface, there was a low peak from which we would see if we would survive or not. We were numb with exhaustion and only half-conscious. The bright snow seemed to penetrate and burn out our reason, attention, hope. Our unit lay frozen two days behind us, lined up in the yard of a burned-out church, their greatcoats over them. We walked strung out, Haas far ahead, myself in the middle, and Grebauer, who had joined us from another lost unit the day before, struggled far behind me. Haas was suspicious of him because he told us that he had seen SS soldiers killing women and children in Siedlce. "These are lies, Bolshevik deceptions," Haas said. Grebauer laughed and continued from time to time to tell these stories, always as if to test the limits of Haas's disbelief. Later Haas whispered to me, "A deserter, I think."

Walking toward the peak, I saw the horizon divide so that there was a blue, boiling space in the center, through which torrents of water rushed. At a point where the water would achieve visual particularity, the strange mass became a multitude of pale horses, their snouts, breath vapor, manes all distinct in the middle distance. Cavalry perhaps. I was about to warn Haas about them when I realized that it was a mirage.

Grebauer marched out of the trench Haas and I had made in the snow and came to rest, looking off toward a shattered tree stump on our left. Then he sat down. "I will rest here, until someone comes," he called to me. Then he laughed. "*Lebensraum*," he said. "We have more than we can use, I think."

"No one will come," I said. "You'll die." He looked small and dirty, sitting there in the snow.

Haas came back to us. "Grebauer, get up." The man laughed, leaning back. "I order you to get up." Grebauer gazed at him as if not comprehending the order.

"One man put a baby's foot on the ground and stepped on it, then pulled it up by the other leg and killed it."

"Get up," Haas said.

"The mother watched. She looked strange, as if she were trying to remember something. A name perhaps." Haas looked thoughtfully at Grebauer, as if he were trying to visualize Grebauer's story.

We got him up and continued to climb in the snow, trudging through the vapor of our breath. Haas was the first to break to the top; then I joined him. Ahead there was a stunning perfection of snow, an infinity of blinding, bluish white under the sky, as if we had emerged on the hilltop to face the vast expanse we had just crossed. Only our trail proved our advance. In the far distance, the horizon was speckled with shimmering lakes and beyond, strange forms, cities of ice, the suggestion of bright onion domes.

Haas reached inside his coat, and I heard a ripping sound. Then he held his insignia in his hand, absurdly dense in color. He blinked at them, his eyes flooding, and dropped them into the snow.

Grebauer was lying behind us. Haas trudged back to him and leaned down. "Come, Grebauer," he said. He lifted the dazed little man and wrapped one arm over his shoulder. "Come, we might be in Poland already. Perhaps only a short distance."

"Here, let me help," I said, taking Grebauer's free arm.

"I feel warm," Grebauer said. "I'm not even cold anymore. The earth underneath is warm to the touch, did you notice?"

"Tell me, my friend," Haas said, plowing into the glittering plain before us, "what else did you see in Siedlce?"

"One would think that the snow would melt, with the earth so warm," Grebauer said.

WESTERN RUSSIA, WINTER 1944
The Ice Unit

We were in a remote area, moving westward as a part of the great Soviet offensive. Some of us wondered as we marched, sometimes achieving twenty kilometers in a single day across difficult terrain, would we ever see a German soldier? Pusev, our commander, was continually disagreeable because, for him, a man with experience in war, this particular set of orders and locations was below his capabilities. "Imagine," he would say, "here I am a veteran of the Great War and numerous campaigns against the Whites, and what do they give me? A bunch of conscripts who don't even shave yet and some ignorant Kazakhs!" We younger conscripts would smile at each other and make fun of the perpetual huff poor Pusev was in. He was insufferably superior to all of us, so much so that his overbearing attitude became a kind of joke.

At length we advanced upon a suspicious-looking area in the brushy, slush-covered outskirts of a deserted railway maintenance station that our unit had secured an hour earlier. There had been nothing to note at the station except evidence of limited occupation: one round mess can of the type German soldiers carry, feces in one corner, a couple of obscure documents with the Wehrmacht crest on top. "Gone already," Pusev said, "and me with my automatic loaded!" But this suspicious area nearby piqued Pusev's curiosity; he was sure soldiers were there. We would now have an engagement. A Kazakh scout was sent to within thirty meters to take a closer look. He moved quickly on his haunches with a kind of animal grace. Then he scrambled back, his broad face beaming with excitement. He had seen the shape of a man, probably a guard. Pusev ordered us to check our weapons, and we advanced. Pusev was the first to get to the Kazakh's forwardmost position. He raised himself up, aimed, and fired a burst, then ducked and rose again. Suddenly he was running back toward us, stepping high through the heavy snow, his face locked in wide-eyed amazement. "I—I—" but he could not speak. The Kazakh scout went along the path in the snow and looked, then stood up and waved us forward.

We found eleven German soldiers, all frozen solid. They had been set up in various statuesque positions, perhaps months ago. The superstitious Kazakhs stayed at the edge of the arrangement of soldiers, talking among themselves, their backs to the display. The sentry that Pusev had shot was sitting there pocked with icy depressions in the face and tunic, his mouth slack and a frozen wound on the side of his head. Behind him five men sat in a circle, their arms up in gestures that are common during conversation. They had been held in these positions with thick stakes and pieces of wire. Another soldier stood straight as a board, at attention. His fly was open and inside we could see the ice-encased genitals. The sculptor had failed to make his hand stay where it was supposed to. Two other soldiers were locked like rigid, expressionless dolls in the attitude of a man and a woman making love, their pants pulled loose and frozen around their rock-hard thighs. One of them had a hand with a missing ring finger hovering over the other's back. "Partisans," Pusev whispered. "They have a detestable sense of humor. Look, they set them up with sticks and wire."

"This happened long ago," I said.

"Yes," Pusev whispered. "See how some of the snow has begun to melt around them." I think that at that moment we all began to feel an uncomfortable chill. We were about to leave when one of the men emerged from behind a bush breathing quickly as if he had been running, a look of grim amazement on his face. I went to him. Behind the bush the partisans had set up two soldiers facing each other on their knees, each with a pistol held at the other's face, and the barrels of the pistols had been jammed each into the other's right eye all the way to the trigger housing. The partisan had apparently had to hammer the barrels into the eye sockets of the dead soldiers. Their faces were locked in icy grins, and their free arms with closed fists were in their laps, with their flies open. This arrangement had required a number of sticks and tightly twisted lengths of wire.

We left the lewd memorial as it was, assuming that the warmer weather would release the men into a more proper rest. We never did become involved in any shooting engagement with German soldiers; in fact, all of those we were to see later would be strewn along roadsides with their personal effects littered around them, or arranged in lines of prone corpses, or hanging from the branches of splintered trees. But Pusev took it all in silence, at least until there was a definite change in the weather.

WESTERN RUSSIA, WINTER 1944
The Orchard

Lev Rogin awakened slowly. There was a sound somewhere, but he could not identify it—a beat of some kind, not synchronized with the rapid beating of his heart. His mouth was full of saliva, and his limbs were numb. He had discovered that those who are starving produce a lot of saliva. He had had no food in days, and, before that, hiding out with other Jews in a small, furnished pit on the outside of a village, he had had only enough food to keep him from becoming sick. But he had been driven nearly mad by the closeness: I need more room. Would you please stop that? How can I help it? What would you do about gas? Don't I eat the same? Well, whose bowels did *you* inherit? Lev Rogin had left one day and wandered into the icy, remote woods, and yesterday he was reduced to crawling into this meager little shack. Death by freezing was alleged to be almost pleasant, and waking up he was not pleased to realize that he was still alive. This business of dying had extended itself to the point that, at twenty, Rogin felt eighty years old.

His heartbeat slowed, and he thought he would get up. But he was already exhausted. The strange ticking came to him again, and this time he caught something in his peripheral vision. Water—it was water dripping off the old wooden roof of the shack. He forced himself to think, and its significance gradually became clear. The circular courses of the planets, the mammoth sweeping of their paths around the sun, had all conspired to break the winter's back. This seemed to mean that there would be another spring. He wanted to see the water, and he struggled to his knees.

The blazing whiteness drove his eyes nearly shut as he crawled. Yes, it was warmer, almost balmy. He ended up at the base of a gnarled tree, ridiculously angular against the riotous blue of the sky. He ate a handful of snow, and in a short while the acidic cramps doubled him over. He rocked with his forearms gripped over his stomach, and saw under him a slab of dirty, blue-black ice with strange cracks in it, creating multicolored sheets that fractured through to the dirt. In these silver sheets were tiny, brilliant points of color, as if the ice were some crystalline mineral. For a moment his eyes were locked on this universe of shape and color, and, because of the weak grasp that his senses had on reality, he seemed to lose his hearing, sense of touch, even his pain. The ice was a tiny spectacle of shifting prismatic variation, which convinced him that, when you are starving to death, it is the eyes that die last.

Then they caught something else, brown circular shapes suspended deep in the ice. Stones, or curled leaves. He drove his fingers under the sharp lip of the ice and broke up a section half a meter square. The strange shapes were embedded on the ground's surface, and he picked at one and broke it out. Realizing that its weight suggested something other than a stone, he brought it to his mouth and bit it. His mouth was stung by an astringent, fermented bitterness, and he chewed the strange brown material for a few seconds, then spat a dark seed into his hand. "Apple," he said. He began to tremble uncontrollably and became dizzy and numb.

Lev Rogin vomited up the first few apples he ate, hoping that his stomach had absorbed some small percentage of the material before sending it up. He ate more, concentrating on doing it slowly, and began to feel juices squirting and organs moving with a painful but harmonious vigor. Then he looked up and saw that beyond this tree was another equally gnarled, and beyond that another, in a straight line that defied chance. He had stumbled into an orchard. He could not control himself, and wept. The only clear conviction that he had had in weeks came to him then: If he could survive, if he managed to make his way through this pain, through this universal orgy of death, then he would spend his life raising apples. He would have every kind, dangling from the limbs of his trees, and even from high in the air in a plane you would see, sweeping below you, the dusky grid of trees studded with a profusion of red dots, and his trees would be laid out with careful geometric precision, and the lines they made would stretch all the way to the horizon.

EASTERN POLAND, WINTER 1944
Another Speculation on Death

I guarded the professor the night before he was shot. It was a painful thing for all of us because we truly respected him and he had a reputation as a humanist and thinker. But our leader, an underground soldier all these years and former officer in the cavalry, had decided that his collaboration, however seemingly harmless, had to be punished. The man had, after all, enriched himself in various ways on the pain of others. He had helped the Nazis identify people "appropriate" for transport to the East. When he realized he was to be shot the next morning, he looked at us sadly but with calm understanding. Of course, what must be done must be done.

The night before the execution, his daughter was permitted to visit him. She was perhaps nine years old, at that age when a grasp of reality is not fully developed. We had the professor chained to a chair in the back of the church, in a store room. Since the Germans were gone, we were able to move about our village more freely.

The professor's daughter looked at him with moon-eyed sympathy. "Are they going to shoot you?"

"Yes," he said, "it seems necessary."

"Will it hurt?"

"No."

"But how will I ever see you if you're dead?"

The professor leaned back in his chair and rattled his chains thoughtfully. Then he said, "When you die, your own awareness ceases, but, as long as there is awareness, then you participate in it. In other words, awareness belongs to the species, and the individual participates. You don't die, the individual 'you' is simply transferred, forgetting all of your life, to the awareness of another. The dead see through the living." The little girl nodded doubtfully, and I considered this explanation. It struck me as a valid idea. Here everyone was trying to explain death, and the professor had presented succinctly one of the best explanations I had heard. "So you participate in the pain, pleasure, and memory of some other individual," he went on. "The nothingness we all fear doesn't exist, in fact cannot exist, unless awareness ceases to exist. So I will participate in your awareness after tomorrow."

"Will I feel it?"

"Perhaps. Just make me happy."

"I will," she said. Then she began to cry. He laughed and told her not to be concerned. He had no fear of death and knew each and every person would someday have to face it. I was a little choked up at all this.

Some fool let the daughter go out when we executed the professor the next day. This would have been all right except for what happened. He was being walked by three partisans to the clearing outside the village, where he was to be shot. He looked serene and loftily sacrificial, almost as if he had become philosophically weary of the procedure. But when they were emerging from the woods toward the spot where other partisans stood by a fence post, the professor began to speak to the men leading him. I could see the fog of his breath shooting out of his mouth. The little girl stood by a brushy hedgerow watching, perhaps wondering if she would be able to feel his perception waft into her brain after his death.

The professor had stopped, and he now began to plead in a loud, whining voice, no, you can't, you mustn't. Please don't, I beg you! I'll do anything! He wrapped his arms around a tree and began to cry with fright and misery. Two partisans had to peel his fingers one by one off the tree and carry him toward the execution post while he squirmed and writhed and bellowed with throat-ripping shrieks. He would not stand at the post, so we tied him around the waist and thighs, and, as we stood back and prepared to shoot, he began to hoot and shout with a combination of laughing and crying, throwing the upper part of his body at us in a series of lunging bows, all the time staring past us with a strange, manic expression on his face. Then it was over.

In the silence following the gunfire, I remembered the little girl. She was there by the hedgerow staring at her father, who now dripped blood into the snow. She was as still as a statue, breath vapor curling away from her pink, expressionless face.

EASTERN GERMANY, SPRING 1944
Against Nature

Brammer had locked himself in a small hangar anteroom and had a PPK with him. We all milled around inside the vast building in small groups, planning ways to draw him back out. His loss of stability was very sudden: I had intended to help him into the Dornier, a simple gesture of friendship, when he had turned and looked at me, his face ashen and distant, as if he no longer knew who I was. Despite our orders, despite the terrible urgency of the situation, he had run back into the hangar. It was sad; Brammer was our best pilot and had distinguished himself over the years with an accumulation of citations none of us could ever match. But he was moody and enigmatic, and I was the only one who felt comfortable addressing him by his first name. We went on our bombing runs without him that day, dropping out those dotted lines of bombs on Russian transport routes and watching the expanding circles of shock waves as they hit. Then we returned, our planes pocked by shrapnel and our feet numb from the cold, tension, and floor vibration. Brammer was still in the anteroom just as we had thought he might be, since our runs had now become frighteningly short—the Russians, it seemed, were closer every day.

When I neared the anteroom, I heard Brammer yelling at us in a voice so hoarse that he sounded like an old man: "Unnatural! It is unnatural! Men are not made for it!"

There was a silence through which our commanding officer glanced frequently at his watch and snapped whispered orders at his men: "We've no time for this neurotic idiocy—get him out. You, check on the aircraft maintenance; we've got to go out again."

"Gravity has a purpose!" Brammer screamed. "We are not made to defy it! Only birds and insects fly!"

"Karl," I called, "please come out. We'll help you."

Again, another silence. Then, in a voice implying some conspiracy on my part, he said in a softer voice, "Ah, it is Noftz—Noftz, the bombardier who has no nerves. My friend, you have been tricked! You think that flying is a simple matter."

"Of course it isn't," I said.

"Ah, so simple. Don't you know what they are doing? Driving fish onto land, birds into the water, moles into treetops!"

We had just begun to laugh at this oddly poetic defense of his mania when we heard the muffled shot. I ran on legs that had no tension and little feeling. Three of us went through the door, I suppose thinking that we might save him despite his wound.

He sat there looking up at us. The PPK was on the floor. "I shot Göring," he said, pointing to the wall. The picture there had a hole in its fat cheek, and the floor glittered with glass fragments. "Our great war ace," Brammer said. "We haven't a plane that can handle all that weight."

We all looked at each other. "Karl," I said, "we still have our orders."

"If I got that fat," he said, "would I be exempt? Is there an obesity exemption?"

"Most certainly," I said. "After all, fuel is scarce."

"But in the meantime, being lean, I must go up."

"You must go up."

"Ah, I see."

NEAR MINSK, SUMMER 1944
The Dead Are Not Hungry

Smelkov leaned against the barbed-wire fence, watching the other prisoners at their preparations for the reprisal. Each man had made some kind of peace with the idea; some prayed, some gazed with an inward-turning speculation at the line of trees down the slope near the river, perhaps imagining somehow running to them and avoiding the bullet that would finally end all this horrible discomfort and this hunger, which ate at them constantly. Smelkov took the news with something like relief—to be released from this torture in a single, hot flash. The prospect of death invited him like a long, dreamless sleep.

Kalinin, the man closest to him at the fence, stared at the gate. "Why are the Germans not here?" he asked.

"They need all their men for the killing," Smelkov said. "This morning they took three hundred. It'll take days."

They had learned of the reprisal the day before. The SS had found the bodies of three of their men in the woods, mutilated and naked. The reprisal would be the execution of four thousand men, and, as the information had rippled through the crowds of prisoners, the mumbling and whispering had risen into a deafening accumulation of screams and wailing. Men had fallen to their knees, invoked the names of saints, pounded the ground with their fists. Later their hunger had become intolerable, and they had shed the last vestiges of humanity and acted like animals—after all, only a day or two left to live, let's at least go with something in our bellies. Some of the weaker men had been set upon at night by prisoners with crude weapons, and

Smelkov could not at first understand the logic of what they had done: They had cut them open and pulled out their livers. Why? Because liver could be chewed easily, unlike muscles. He had heard of incidents like this before, stories from other camps and from the famines after the Great War. The thought of it frightened him because, thin and weak as he was, he could be the next source of their food.

Smelkov looked at Kalinin's hands. The dirt under the nails had that dark reddish-brown hue, telling him that Kalinin had participated directly. Yesterday, late in the night, he had given three little sticky scraps to Smelkov, who had eaten them quickly lest he think about it too long. But the bitter taste had been almost worse than the hunger.

"Stop looking at me!" Kalinin said. "The poor fellow was nearly dead anyway! Anyway, we knocked him out first." He paused, and Smelkov looked at the gray stubble on his emaciated head.

"Yes, I know," he said.

Kalinin was thinking. "Why do we hear no shots?"

"I don't know. They may have invented another method."

Not a bullet? he wondered. What other ways were there? Clubbing? Drowning? The thought of some more painful method made Smelkov tremble. It was unfair. He looked again toward the gate. In the distance, shimmering inside a cloud of dust, he could see men marching toward the camp, shuffling along in dirty gray smocks. "Prisoners?" he asked. "They seem to be coming back."

Kalinin looked, too. The column of men moved toward the camp as slowly and looking as weak and fatigued as when they had left to be shot.

"What's happening?"

They heard yelling from the gate. The word spread quickly back through the crowds of men. The Germans were gone. The Russians were only a few kilometers away. The men had seen tanks, dust, and glints of light. The ground had shuddered with the rumble of powerful engines.

The discovery that they were to be spared caused a reaction similar to that caused by the news that they were to be shot. Men fell to their knees, prayed, invoked the names of saints, and wept with seeming misery. Smelkov moved as if in a fog, not knowing what to do—free, he was free. Although he felt the subtle, weak surge of a kind of joy, he realized that he had to be careful or he would faint. The light-headedness kept him at the fence, holding onto the wire for support. He felt a strange uneasiness and growing nausea, as if he wanted to retch his insides out. He began to sweat.

Kalinin seemed unable to move. He sat by the fence staring with glassy eyes at the dirt before him, saying something to himself over and over.

"What? What's the matter?" Smelkov said.

Kalinin was weeping, holding his hands to his face.

"Did you hear? We're to be liberated!" Smelkov said.

But Kalinin looked up at him, his face drawn with astonishment and growing fright.

"I have eaten human flesh," he whispered. "Dear God, I have eaten human flesh."

WESTERN RUSSIA, SUMMER 1944

Stress

The orders had come down. We were to eliminate ten thousand Russian prisoners in a matter of thirty-six hours. Sturmbannführer Kleist had already shown signs of severe hypertension, and we felt that this order would be his undoing. To make matters worse, some SS men had deserted our little camp, and we were left with only fifty men, along with a group of well-trusted Kapos, whom we were to eliminate when the task of killing the Russians was completed. One of these Kapos, a little Hungarian criminal named Jan Rozsca and nicknamed by our unit "The Rat" because of his pointed, rodentlike face, showed in his behavior a kind of hysterically ingratiating attitude, signifying that he knew what our orders meant as far as his life was concerned. "Yes," he would say, peering up at me with a look of conspiratorial brotherhood on his ferocious, ratlike face, "a difficult task to be sure! And burning the corpses! Ah! If they only knew how difficult this is!"

To add to his misery, Rozsca had an ugly, infected wound in the palm of his hand, and, during the weeks of reports of the Russian advance, it got worse, to the point where his sore became his one obsession. He would hold his hand aloft all day, and we would see him ruefully poking his armpit, searching the swollen lymph glands there for evidence of the infection's progress. Like Sturmbannführer Kleist, he showed his stress. His face would be twisted into a miserable, obsequious smile, and he would poke his armpit and then suddenly become overexcited and make another ridiculous suggestion as to how to solve the problem of the crowd of hungry, tattered Russians. "Perhaps we should get flamethrowers and simply fry them on the spot! I've seen it done!"

"We have no flamethrowers."

"Ah! It is difficult, to be sure!"

"We're going to build wood pyres and shoot them and then burn the bodies."

"Wood pyres! Almighty God!" I could see his face bead with nervous sweat. He smiled with a look of beseeching complicity, his hand held over his head. "I'll help—I can kill more of these beggars in a day than any man!" This was true. Like many Kapos, his life depended on obedience and usefulness; when it came to killing Russians, the Rat already had a good record. "I am valuable to you, no?"

"To be sure," I said. He laughed, and the arm drooped from fatigue. He winced and fingered his armpit.

"I must wash this again," he said. His wrist was already splotched red, and the brooding look on his face, that gaze of intense desire, seemed to show him halting the infection by an act of will. "You'll see," he said, "the human body is an amazing thing. This will pass."

Sturmbannführer Kleist walked over to us. "Trucks are bringing the wood, and we have a few recruits from the Viking Division." He was pale and drawn and looked to be on the edge of cracking. "You, Rat," he said to Rozsca, "gather your men and bring the prisoners out by twenties."

"Yes, sir," the Rat said. Since his hand was already raised, he simply tensed it in salute and went to the barracks.

"I want four extra men with machine pistols to oversee this," Kleist said. "The Rat knows."

I would estimate that we killed only four or five hundred Russians before we were forced to retreat. Kleist did crack: We found him one morning screeching at the crowd of frightened Russians, "I order you to die! I order you filthy devils to stop breathing! Die! Die, goddammit!" We convinced him to drink half a bottle of Jägermeister, and after that he was all right. I was very concerned about him.

We left without burning the last of the pyres of forty bodies, each shot in the back of the neck and stacked in with the logs that oozed a fragrant, amber sap. It was my job to eliminate the Rat, and I did so at a moment of lull while one fire was just beginning to singe the short hair on the heads of the last group that we managed to burn. I slipped up behind him while he worked his finger in his armpit with his right hand held up and shot him just below the point at the base of the skull. He turned as he fell, and I left him lying there with his right hand still up. His face was relaxed for the first time since I had known him. The wound on his hand had nearly healed. He had apparently managed to beat his infection. Sad.

NEAR PINSK, SUMMER 1944
The Beast of the Marshes

We had invented the name "The Beast of the Marshes" in reference to a deranged partisan who became so effective in his assaults against us that, for a while, we easily lapsed into the secret conviction that this one man was the principal objective of our war. No matter how extensive the reprisals against the civilian population—women and children hanging by their necks from crude jibs—he struck again and again, each time in a manner more frightfully perverse than the last. The partisan's calling card was a single tooth, sometimes with gold fillings intact. He would tie the tooth into the knot that bound the string around one kind of box or another containing the proof of his hideous deeds. And he would always place the box in a location suggesting the hopeless vulnerability of our defenses. Once Standartenführer Haupt found on the doorstep of his billet an ornate box of the type women keep silver brushes in. The tooth had been wound inside the knot holding the box closed. Inside the box, lying on thick blue velvet, he found six strips of dark flesh, which a young former medical student identified as lips. Six lips. This discovery corresponded with information that a number of our guards had disappeared within the previous two days. We kicked stools and blocks of wood out from under the feet of fifteen peasants that day, but the message was apparently unconvincing, for on the next day Standartenführer Haupt found a hatbox on the billet doorstep, and before he opened it he could feel the contents shifting from one side to the other in a slow and noiseless change of weight distribution. Inside were the genitals of four men. Perhaps most horrible of all was the problem of numbers. Six lips meant three men, but here we had proof of four victims. Standartenführer Haupt looked out over the flat expanse at the edge of the huge, forbidding Pripet marshes and informed us that, under the circumstances no reprisals would be carried out this day. Then he took the box into his office.

"Infants!" Haupt shrieked one day a week later, after we had received our latest gift: The very absurdity of the beast's new counter-offensive seemed to require extraordinary measures. Our medical student identified the contents of the box as kneecaps, five of them. Why the odd number? Why, for that matter, kneecaps? In this case, we found the bodies of the three soldiers not more than a kilometer into the marsh, all shot in the face, along with the mutilation of their knees. Haupt was ashen with fright and rage. "We will need six infants!" This duty was the most difficult I ever performed. Johann Dukas, a good friend of mine, was driven nearly out of his mind by it. When we had finished our gruesome reprisal, he found a single golden hair on his black tunic, and, holding it up to the blazing Russian sun, he burst into tears, now one with the mothers of the tiny children who were swinging in a line under the long portable gallows.

In time we began to see our own haggard troops emerging from the marsh, having retreated westward, transporting their matériel on wooden rails built for the purpose of getting the heavy equipment across the treacherous terrain. They, too, had stories: a piece of wire in a circle passed through the eyeballs of men lost, the tooth at the knot, a small box of nipples, and everywhere the rich stink of carrion. And reprisals? We had run out of peasants, it seemed. Visibly shaken, Standartenführer Haupt read out the list of the missing and surely dead by the hand of the monster. Then he looked at us and said, "Gentlemen, war breeds the most unnatural of creatures. We have been victims of one of them. This beast is human, yes, but the degree of his bestiality has proven to us the barbaric potential in the soul of men. I suppose we will never catch him, and it is perhaps proper that this should be so. He therefore remains the enigmatic symbol of the cruel inhumanity we have tried to contravene."

Our retreat began shortly after this day. Either on foot or in the slow, heavy trucks, many of us, I am sure, confused the reasons for our massive flight. It was as if our escape was not from the Russians but rather from that mysterious horror residing in the character of one person hidden in the swamp, the Beast of the Marshes.

NEAR MINSK, SUMMER 1944
Shell Shock

We knew that Belov had been suffering from a strange disorientation for weeks. Once, during a lull in the fighting, I had peeked into his pack and found the butterflies. They were mounted between square pieces of cardboard with little frames made of tiny twigs so as not to crush their delicate bodies or disturb the fine, bright dust of their wings. The twigs, I discovered, had been lashed together with human hair, and, since we were all cropped closely, I had concluded that Belov had used hairs from his armpits.

One can have little idea of the stress involved in long-term close contact with artillery, both sent out and incoming. The constant shock waves tend to reduce the brain to confused jelly, and Belov had been an artillery gunner longer than any man I knew. I had been in the unit only two months and had already experienced periods of extreme stress; during those times all I could hear was a strange rush of thunderous silence—a contradiction, yes, but true. All I needed in order to understand Belov was to exaggerate my own experience. We would say something after a long trade of artillery with the Germans, and he would stare at us, his eyes focusing at some odd distance between us, and then walk off, most of the time to nearby woods or marshes. We would sit and wait for the pistol report signifying that he had killed himself.

Our unit commander said to me one day, "He is going off the deep end and will soon be a hazard to the operation. Follow him—I think he's going to kill himself this time."

He headed for a patch of high brush, carrying his pack. The protracted tension had reduced many to a kind of temporary imbecility before him, but Belov had hung on, slamming shells into the cannon breech all day and all night. Because of my own fatigue, I wondered if suicide might be a good alternative. We all must die anyway.

Belov made his way into the brush, looking from side to side with a kind of unself-conscious casualness. I was sure he did not know I was following. From his pack he drew a little net on a stick and waited for his prey.

This experience was interesting to me because, as I worked my way through the brush, swinging branches from my path, I noticed the dreamlike silence of everything and felt a beautiful distance from the war. I did see a yellow butterfly, standing on a shiny leaf and slowly fanning its wings to the sun. I was momentarily riveted: The wings were perfect, with brown dots and colorful shapes, and there was that stunning symmetry, like placing a mirror perpendicular to a design. At that moment I felt I understood Belov.

Later, at the camp, when we knew we had to return to our punishment, those erect barrels and the shiny shells stacked nearby, I felt my head tighten in anticipation of the impact of the first blasts. There was a hand on my shoulder. It was Belov, smiling at me with a look of demented complicity. I looked to our commanding officer and shrugged with doubt. He nodded as if to say, it's all right—humor him. Belov led me to a truck where he had stored his pack. He drew a small wooden box from it and gave it to me. Inside was one of the yellow butterflies. I am fairly strong and generally in control of my emotions, but at this moment, hearing behind me the first powerful explosions of the cannons and feeling the tangible power of their shocks rip through my body, I was unable to stop myself; looking down at that beautiful shape, the balance of such forces, I unaccountably began to cry.

This is how Belov survived the war. I have kept the little box with the butterfly in it ever since. Belov seemed always to need to increase the size of his collection, but this one seemed sufficient for me.

NEAR FÜRSTENBURG, GERMANY, SUMMER 1944

Three Soldiers

Sitting on the bluff by the dead soldier's cave, Karl looks out over the neat rows of vegetables tilled by the Russian prisoners and fingers the orders in his pocket. He wonders what is keeping the Russians from their singing today. The line of trucks had appeared on the eastern horizon as he and Kilian had expected, and had parked a hundred meters apart along the rows of vegetables. Dark figures had dropped from the holes in the backs of the canvas-topped beds while the guards had watched, their Mausers pointing toward the ground. Now it has been an hour, and Kilian has wandered off, bored.

The two of them had played out much of their childhood in these woods and had discovered the Russians a year ago; the prisoners would sing as they worked, with such force and multitonal complexity, in that Slavic minor key, that the two boys finally had preferred it to any other music. The mystical Eastern sound of it, along with the deep, uncivilized force of the voices, was awesome.

"I heard that we won't have to go even past the Polish border to fight them," Kilian says from the other side of the cave.

"Good," Karl says. "We'll get to it earlier then."

He rises and goes into the cave. It is only a low hole in the side of the bluff and contains the remains of a soldier from the Great War, probably an escaped Russian from the Tannenberg battle. They had discovered him years ago as children and had kept his existence secret. He had no rifle or helmet, only the rotted remains of a uniform, and small boots. The skeleton was spread all over the shallow cave. One of Karl's habits was to sit and stare into the neck hole of the skull, into the black sphere of space where the man's thought and memory had been. He does this now, holding the light, dry skull in both hands, waiting for the deep sound of the voices.

"Karl!" Kilian whispers. "Something's wrong!"

He goes to the edge of the bluff. In the distance, in sunlight warped by the boiling heat of the morning, he sees a guard striking a prone prisoner with the butt of his rifle. The other men work on, some stumbling, some looking back and working away from the guard and the prone man.

"Why are they—" Karl stops, squinting. The prisoner is dragged toward one of the trucks. He cannot stand. The guard raises the rifle, muzzle up, and strikes him three more times with the butt.

"They'll kill him!" Kilian whispers.

"We'd better leave. If we're seen—"

"But they'll kill him!"

They watch as the men work on. Their hearts thump, and their mouths are full of the taste of metal. Finally, they rise to leave.

Karl pauses by the cave, fingers the papers again, and thinks, which front? Where do they send sixteen-year-olds? He kneels at the cave and rolls the skull back inside into position, opposite the boots.

He turns to his friend. "Wait." He cocks his ear and listens for voices, but there is only the hollow sound made by the wind in the trees.

NEAR ARNHEM, HOLLAND, FALL 1944
Making Contact

Dirlewanger waited while the Dutch contacts took his papers into another room, toward the back of the dingy farmer's cottage. He was not sure if he was in Holland, but it didn't matter as long as the papers were acceptable to the partisans. He tried to relax, to capitalize on the opportunity to rest, but his temples throbbed and his hands were tight, sweaty fists in his lap. He had walked and begged short rides all across Germany, and the journey was made into a monumental struggle because he had carried more than forty kilograms of unrefined dental gold in leather pillows bound around his body. Walking like a normal human being had required considerable athletic skill. His undergarments had chafed his armpits and crotch raw, his legs ached horribly, and his heart pounded with dangerous force.

The act of deserting his fatherland, sacrificed by military ineptitude and high-command corruption, had seemed awful to him. Beyond that, he would never in his life be able to get over the horror of standing before hundreds of kilograms of dental gold, fillings that glittered among tooth scraps and yellowed plaque, and knowing that there was no way he would ever be able to carry it. But he had sneaked out with his forty kilos shortly before the massive, bleak extermination camp had been dismantled, and had got rid of his SS uniform just inside the border of eastern Germany.

Sitting in the cottage, Dirlewanger was sure his deception would work. He had used the name of one Geradus Schneck, a Dutchman who at the camp had worn the inmate's green triangle signifying that he was a criminal. His photograph resembled Dirlewanger so closely that it would take an expert to know the difference. Dirlewanger had interrogated Schneck at the camp, using the usual truncheon blows and finger twisting, and had extracted the necessary information. Schneck was now, of course, a cloud, by necessity. Dirlewanger's desire to get out of the war had been recognized by Schneck, who, it seemed, had wanted to barter the information and papers in order to save his own miserable skin. It amused Dirlewanger that two of the gold teeth now being warmed by his body heat came from Schneck's mouth. The stupid man! He had finally informed Dirlewanger that he himself wanted passage to America, and he knew how he could get it. Dirlewanger, aware of the photograph, had known that Schneck's revelation was his own way out. When Dirlewanger had indicated that it was Schneck's time to die, Schneck had tried the last ploy and had revealed the names of the men on the border of Holland who could arrange the flight. But he had known it was useless to try and barter and had come out finally with a wan, hopeless shrug, and had laughed with dejected abandon just as Dirlewanger had the Kapo wind the thin garrote around his neck.

He waited. The gold, which felt like bags of sand, encased his lower trunk, and he hoped only that the men would find no excuse to search him.

They returned to the room smiling, one holding the papers. "Geradus Schneck," one said.

"Yes," Dirlewanger said.

"You are under arrest," the man turned and looked at the other man, "by our—say, organization here. There are a couple of small villages that you must pay for."

After the brutal search, the discovery of the gold, and the beating that followed, there was a conversation during which Dirlewanger tried to convince them that he was not Geradus Schneck—"Of course you're not! Of course! A murderer of children like you! You're obviously someone else and photographs lie! We are going to hang someone else tomorrow! Of course!" It came to Dirlewanger gradually, while he shook his head at their accusations and wiped the blood from his mouth and nose, that the crafty Schneck, criminal, conspirator, and collector of campbound Jews' valuables belonging legally to the Reich, had after all had the presence of mind, all beaten up and bloody as he was, to barter wisely—a life for a life.

WESTERN POLAND, FALL 1944
Last Engagement

We had been separated from our command for two days and were halted by even the smallest rivers because our own troops had dynamited all the bridges during the retreat. Kassler, an expert rifleman and tank gunner and somewhat famous veteran of panzer battles against Yeremenko in the South, had abandoned his machine as I had mine, and we had resurrected a damaged half-track to take us back home. As we went, Kassler looked about, amazed at the destruction. "A little barn," he would say, pointing, "why burn a peasant's little barn? A pile of hay?"

"A few years ago the Russians did it, too," I said, more than once.

And he would say something like, "Fall is beautiful here. You know, before the war I was a locksmith."

Our conversations had little in the way of serious content because

Kassler seemed so distant most of the time. And because, in our sleepless flight from the advancing Russians, we were exhausted; we remained alert only because of our fear.

Somewhere near the border, west of the city of Posen, we reached the top of a knoll and scanned the countryside, looking for rivers that would make our means of transportation useless. But the flat land streamed off into the distance, lush and verdant. To our right we saw a village in a hollow. The spire of the church was untouched, with the dense silhouette of the bell at its lower end. "Pretty, no?" Kassler said. Then he tipped his head and turned the engine off. "Listen."

We could hear the partisans celebrating in a steady din of singing and hooting. The village seemed remarkably well preserved considering the destruction we had just crossed, the burned machinery and bloated horses, wrecked buildings. We could see human movement around the center of the little village and animals grazing in the fields at its perimeters.

Kassler reached down next to his seat and drew out his Mauser.

"No," I said. "Don't, there's no point."

"They celebrate too quickly," he said.

"Don't." But because of my fatigue I couldn't stop him, and I stared at the rifle, mesmerized by the stupidity of the act.

Kassler adjusted the scope very carefully, whispering to himself, estimating distance and trajectory. Then he draped himself over the windshield frame and set his aim. I watched his face relax its tension, his finger slowly drawing the trigger.

He fired. In about a second, the sound of the bell's ringing came back. "What?" I said.

Kassler waved his arm, threw the bolt, set his aim, and again rang the bell. This time the partisans identified us and faded for cover. Frightened, I began to rummage on the floor of the half-track for machine-gun ammunition.

Kassler started the engine. "It is all right for me to help them celebrate," he said. "You see, I am a German, certainly, but from now on my nationality shall be 'locksmith.' Can one do that?"

"I don't know," I said. I looked back to see if we were being followed, but the road was empty. Then Kassler poked my shoulder, making me flinch with fright. "What? What?"

"Look there," he said. "Those trees! Fall is beautiful, no?"

CENTRAL POLAND, WINTER 1945

The Animated Dead

I had the sheet wrapped tightly around me as I walked and so was not in any danger from what I saw. Even the corpses that had been mutilated beyond recognition moved to the rhythmic cadence of their evil directives, and I was afraid at times that it was my presence that caused them to move. I approached a village that I dimly recognized; smoke rose from the roofs of the houses, curling around huge, somnolent birds of prey, and vehicles, many bearing the gray double cross of the Nazi army, littered the ditches on either side of the road. I pulled the sheet tighter, knowing the ridicule I would have to endure. But I had to confront them, and, anyway, the sheet guaranteed me safety. I had to locate my husband and children.

At the first of the village houses, I saw on a porch a German soldier with part of his face gone copulating with a young girl who had been hanged. Her skin seemed almost bluish it was so pale, and the bruise on her neck led on one side to a small pinch wound, apparently made by the knot of her rope. The German, busy at his work, paid no attention to me, but the dead girl spat thick, bloody saliva in my direction and laughed with a humiliating shriek. I held the sheet to my breast and walked on.

Toward the village center, there were more of the happy, gregarious dead. Even the most shy and wistful-looking of them behaved badly, particularly the girls, lifting their skirts, throwing feces and frozen body parts in my direction, spitting, baring and shaking their breasts, and shouting curses. But the sheet protected me. I decided to look in the church.

The dead have no inhibitions and look on the living with vicious, condescending scorn. They like to desecrate sacred places, and so I was not surprised at what I saw there: wine bottles littering the vestibule, corpses sleeping naked in the pews, an adolescent boy and an old woman engaged in fatigued, doglike copulation under the cross, watched over by a dead priest who read the Bible upside down, his piercing voice mocking it furiously. The cross was marred with carved obscenities. Someone had hung a baby by its foot near the small, ornate organ, and it peered at me from its inverted position with a strange, gaping smile. I had to turn to see if it was one of my own but stopped, realizing that my children had been older.

I left the church. I noticed that dust and filth had begun to soil the sheet, and I walked on out the other end of the village. It was growing dark, and I was afraid of being confused as to my location. Finally I decided that they were lost, all four of them. Perhaps it is better that I could not find them now. Since they had joined that rabble of nearly infinite number and had adopted their evil ways, I feared the thought of what they would be doing if and when I did find them. Outside the village I saw an old woman apparently digging onions, and, happy to have encountered one of the shrinking legion of the living, I approached her, but she looked at me in horror and hobbled away, crossing herself and leaving a trail of small onions behind her.

NEAR LODZ, POLAND, SPRING 1945
Sniper's War

Today there are sounds of jubilation in the distance. A welcoming group of partisans emerges from the village and moves in my direction. Behind them, villagers cheer the advancing Russians just as they had thought it best to cheer the Germans years ago and then the partisan groups when they had raided the town at night in search of supplies and comfort. I have waited on the perimeter of this village three days, and my partisan contact, an emaciated man with thick glasses and hands so arthritic that they look like crushed spiders, has come once, with food and warning: We shall start normal life once more, and the communists are our saviors.

Since the first lightning blow of the Germans, I have lived a life of movement and solitude. One forced into these circumstances develops isolated forms of genius. In my case, it is the full understanding of the properties of my Mauser and the perfection of my craft, including my discovery of the mysterious tricks of camouflage; in a plain as flat and vast as my country's, there is no place to hide, so that, according to the principle of inversion, no one can find me. My life is a movement across a shimmering plain in search of targets: the black-uniformed SS, the mustard-colored soldiers. I float my target in the circle of liquid light crossed by the hairs and watch him drop on the boiling horizon. The report fills the sky with divine applause, a hollow chorus of angels' voices. Satisfied, I retreat into the distance, avoiding sparse woodland and streambeds where I will be looked for. I clean and oil the Mauser and inspect it closely for evidence of wear or rust, knowing that the reprisal for one target's death is dozens of villagers hanged, turning in the breeze.

Only rarely have I been forced to approach my targets, when they fought death, clawing at the wound made by an imperfect shot. When they have looked up at me with that lucidity bred by pain, I have realized the full genius of the mechanism—to throw metal at such speed!

I study the approaching villagers through the scope, while, in the foreground of the liquid circle, hay stubble shimmers in the sun. I sweep the circle over thatch houses, seeking appropriate targets: a dog, a child, a military vehicle. Behind the village, clouds of dust mark the advance of the Russians. Now the contingent of villagers fills the circle. They are led by the arthritic partisan. I slide back, dragging my pack on the ground. Then I sit and wait for the imperfections of muscular control to fade and for the eye to become one with the magical device that swallows distance up. The largest man drops on the horizon in a dreamlike limpness, while the rest scatter in surprise. The sky fills with divine applause.

BERLIN, SPRING 1945
The Scholar

I had received communication from one of the Reichsführer's highest and most trusted men that a major collection of runic artifacts had been discovered in a small town in the North. I was ordered to go immediately to examine the Germanic script, those twenty-four angular symbols that objectify the magnificence of our past. My function was research into the history of our race, and as I drove I felt in my hands and face that strange, tingling sensation of intellectual expectation. Devastation marred the land. Berlin's outlying warehouses and factories were blackened, skeletal ruins, and daily the bombings continued. Reports came of our losses in the East, of a massive and ugly wave of Slavic assault on our borders. Saddened as I was by the cataclysmic setback my fatherland now had to endure, I nevertheless pressed on, my heart made strong by the importance I suspected lay in the discovery of the artifacts. Can one assess the magnitude of this pursuit? To drive deeper and deeper into the core of our genealogical identity, to be pulled as if by a magnet toward the glowing evidence of collective self-knowledge.

At length I advanced upon a long column of people shuffling slowly across the road I traveled. I had to pull the car to a halt. This curious, seemingly endless column was apparently a group of prisoners, herded by army guards, and, as I focused on them, I saw that these people were unbelievably unkempt; there wafted from them in the breeze the horrific odor of human oppression and filth. They looked like the walking dead. I got out of my car. Who were they? Russians? Criminals? Jews? A young officer marched past, saluted me with nearly insulting casualness, and stopped to light a cigarette.

"Are these people not a health hazard?" I asked.

He laughed, blowing smoke—a rude and presumptuous young man.

I heard a shot and, out of the corner of my eye, observed to my horror another officer holstering a pistol, having just shot a prisoner who had apparently straggled off to the side of the road.

"The women can't make it," the young man said.

"A woman?" I was confused by this. "Would you have your unit shoot women?"

"Oh, we shoot everyone," he said, and then laughed with a kind of barbaric abandon.

"I demand to know what is going on here."

"Oh, do you?"

I was now angry, about to reach for my pistol, perhaps to shoot him forthwith. But I was unused to such practices. My place, after all, was a familiar cone of yellow light in which I studied old manuscripts, books. "Your insolence astounds me," I said, finally. He nodded thoughtfully, dropped his cigarette. I heard another shot.

"Minus another," he said. "Yes, this is the remnant of the Jewish race—kings and princesses, rabbis and philosophers—"

"But—"

"—great thinkers, musicians—"

"Stop it," I said. "Where are you taking them?"

"To their new promised land, courtesy of the Reich."

"Stop being vague."

He laughed again and walked off.

Dumbfounded as I was, I could think of nothing else to do but watch the line of animated corpses as it passed. Perhaps it had been meddling on my part to have confronted the young man. Perhaps some military necessity was being carried out. Was it right for me to question his orders? Obviously not. I sighed and looked beyond the line toward some still-bare trees in the middle distance. Their angular branches suggested to me cryptic symbols, meaningful shapes, which it was my duty to study. This is, after all, the secret to a useful life: to pursue, despite such shocking distractions as I had just witnessed, my great goal. I halted a guard and ordered him to break the line for me. He did so, raising the people he stopped out of their dumb stupor and causing a chain reaction of those behind bumping into each other, closing the line like sticks being pushed together. Thus I repaired to my car and continued my journey north.

DACHAU, APRIL 1945
Liberation

The prisoners are all crowded out in the Lagerstrasse, while, inside the block, prisoner Koch sits with five corpses, the previous night's dead, and with Silber, an emaciated survivor too weak to join the crowd outside. The Americans are liberating the camp, and Koch is unable to think of what to do next. He retreats into fascination with the images of the dead. They are skin-covered skeletons with bald heads and hairless faces set in a pale and marbled stillness suggesting that they are, as he has observed before, all identical now, having shed the imperfections of individuality. They have changed to a different life form. His own body is like theirs but as yet not fully transformed.

"They're out there," Silber says. In spite of his weakness, he is able to communicate a forceful mockery. Koch shakes his head slowly; how often he has had to endure their jests.

"You don't understand—none of you do."

"Do you have the strength to do it?" Silber asks. "Americans are very big, you know, as big as your Germans."

"Fool," Koch whispers. He tries not to listen. After all, it is his business if he wants to kill an American.

"They'll be sending food soon now," Silber says. "You'd better get your strength up."

"You may have mine," Koch says. "I'll have no need for it."

Silber shakes his head in apparent exasperation. "So where are your idols now?"

Where? Koch wonders—the inverse gods in their black uniforms executing their secret mission. He lapses into recollection: In his previous camp in the East, he was at first beaten, tortured for no reason, and then gradually battered down into a thin sheet of devoted and obedient tin. Before that, he had failed to see his oppressors as higher beings engaged in a mission that few understood. The execution of this mission had reached its stunning zenith when his masters had killed the Hungarians, hundreds of thousands of them in a matter of weeks, so that mammoth fire pits billowing with voluptuous smoke had charred the corpses into fine ash. Koch had ladled boiling human fat from collecting reservoirs and poured it back over the unburned corpses, coughing and choking in the powerful, acrid smoke, while all around the pits, servants like him had moved the corpses with pitchforks. He knew the secret regardless of the others' skepticism: It was the transformation of useless human fodder; the hairless domes of heads, the identical features, the nakedness—they are the dormant, embryonic forms, like those of insects, waiting to develop into some invisible imago, being readied for release out of the chimneys and fire pits.

"These embryonic forms are resurrected," he whispers.

"You told us that foolishness before," Silber says.

"I wasn't talking to you."

"I was talking to *you*."

Koch rises from his bunk, angry and feeling suddenly potent. Just one—perhaps to wrench his rifle from him and—

"Don't do this," Silber says. Koch detects sympathy in his voice. "You have survived, you have a chance to live now. It's all right to stop this now."

"I have to," he whispers.

"I will hold your food for you."

Outside, he enters the throng of excited men, the tangle of arms, the jostling and the crush of movement.

"Koch!" a voice says. He looks up. It is Weiss, beaming at him from the sea of faces. Koch dismisses him with a wave of his hand and struggles on, noticing that Weiss is now pointing at him and talking jovially to another man.

It takes Koch a seeming eternity to work his way across the Appellplatz to where the Americans are grouped. When he arrives, exhausted, he selects and measures his foe, an older one who has not shaved. His uniform is green and rumpled and smeared with dirt, his helmet marred at the edges. But the futility of the plan overwhelms Koch, and he sags, his will fading; all that is left is one final steel-hard thread of anger, but it is enough to sustain him. He waits, gathering his strength, and lunges. He is too weak, and the American takes it as an expression of his adoration. Koch ends up on his knees, staring down at a bar of chocolate in his hand.

CENTRAL POLAND, SPRING 1945
A Family

Wojtasik had already started the fire, and, lowering himself to his knees, he shook off the last twinges of hesitation and began to fry it on a curved piece of truck fender. Then he heard moans through the wall. He jumped with fright, then checked his rifle—it was loaded. With his eyes still on the purplish carcass, he held his breath. A rape? Or a person dying? The brick wall where he had set up his little camp was high and thick, that of a slaughterhouse. The town had seemed empty, since little was left standing after the Germans' retreat, but then, those close to death would be stuck here. The moans subsided, and he turned again to the carcass. Death, rape—what difference did it make? Those had become, after all, the main products of the machinery of this war. As a man a few years younger, he would never have believed that by this time he would have seen so many hundreds of corpses, in all forms of mutilation and decomposition. In the entire process, he had killed but one man, with a rifle shot.

His hands trembled in a combination of repugnance and anticipation, while his mouth filled with saliva. He would not eat the entrails. No. Only the muscles, the almond-shaped shoulder and flank muscles above the little paws meshed by tiny ribbons of sinew. The complexity of its musculature had startled him when he had pulled off and discarded the slick jacket of gray-furred skin, and he could not clean the carcass because he did not trust his hands to obey him. In his mind, he tried to refuse to hear the awful echo of that word: rat. Again he experienced the acid stab of hunger piercing upward into his chest, making beads of sweat erupt from his face—then, the familiar swoon of dizziness. No. Not the entrails. All but the entrails. The bread he had in his mess can was a bit of luck that may have saved him; it looked so much like a chunk of seat padding that the lost, wounded, starving people emerging from the forests at the rumor of liberation had paid no attention to it lying on the ground.

The moans beyond the wall now sounded more forceful. Cautiously, Wojtasik reached out and felt the hard, reassuring stock of the rifle. But then it was only a woman. He turned again to the carcass and flipped it over, and it spluttered on the fender piece. He would do it soon; he could already smell it, a combination of cooking meat tinged with the metallic odor of viscera. *Only the muscles*. But those sounds: It was as if the woman were trying to lift something, perhaps being pinned under rubble. Curious, he turned away from the carcass and listened. No men's voices. Perhaps death throes. His impulse was to move away, not to intrude on her final moments on this earth. You could do so little for the dying anyway, and the assumption that she was dying was a subtle reassurance. It was not his business. Anyway, the carcass was nearly done; time to let it cool and to go somewhere to eat it. But a strange uneasiness invaded him, as if he were at the brink of some odd and unexpected addition to all he had witnessed. He had to get away.

The baby cried with a faint, rasping sound, like uncontrollable coughing. Wojtasik was suddenly very still there on his knees, shocked and unable to move, staring at the rat. His senses had turned in on themselves, and he saw himself as if from a great distance, a tiny speck on the curved surface of the mutilated earth. *I am only a man*, he thought, *only a man*. But the sensation did not leave him, and his eyes flooded.

He found her in the corner of a large room with half a roof, and butchers' tables and sinks against the wall. She was small and ashen and bathed in sweat, holding the baby to her breast, next to the emaciated rippling of her ribs. She looked to be near death. When she opened her eyes, she looked up at him with bleary comprehension and a strange, ancient patience.

"Bread," he said, holding it out to her. "Here, you must eat." She did, testing it, gazing to his left. He heard the little popping sounds of the baby sucking. "Your husband?"

"I am not married. I—I was assaulted."

The baby was still for a moment. The woman looked at it, then at the floor around her.

"Here," he said. "Wrap it—here." He pulled a thick undershirt from his pack. "It isn't clean, but—"

She struggled up on one elbow. With all the rubble and filth around, there was no place to put the baby. Wojtasik saw that it was a girl and looked healthy and that somehow the woman had already cut and tied off the cord. She wrapped it in the shirt. "Here," he said. "I'll put it—" The tables, no. Wojtasik took the baby with exaggerated gentleness because he had never held one before and rested it in a small porcelain sink. "There," he said. "She won't fall out of that."

The woman looked at his pack. He understood. With his back to her and his hands trembling almost uncontrollably, he pulled out the carcass of the rat and tore the little muscles away from the shoulders and flanks. He gave her these little pieces of meat.

After eating the first bits she said, "Strange, what is this?"

"It is a squirrel," he said.

NEAR ZARY, POLAND, SPRING 1945
Execution of a Collaborator

We walk behind Jasinski, and women emerge from their houses, brooms and switches in their hands. They approach with caution and lash out quickly, and Jasinski waves their brooms and sticks away as if waving away flies. The hole intended for him is at the edge of the village. He is the last collaborator we will shoot, and then we must wait for the Russians. They will be here tonight or tomorrow. The first wave is said to be battle hardened and will not cause us harm. The second wave is said to be a rabble bent on rape and looting. And we fear that, because we are so close to the border, they will confuse us with Germans.

Ahead, Katya emerges from her yard, walking along with a flat shovel in her right hand. She draws our eyes because of her beauty,

Jasinski's because of his fear, mine particularly because years ago, as children—down in the wheat in the glassy and blistering summer afternoons—we two discovered that secret dimension of life locked in tense and sweat-slicked embrace.

Jasinski slows, turns, and whispers a soft protest. We nudge him on, and he steps quickly past Katya, but her movement is so swift that we cannot restrain her, for she is strong and not afraid of Jasinski. She swings the shovel in a quick arc, holding it like an ax, and with the shovel edge shatters Jasinski's shin. He falls into the dirt, holding his leg, tears blinding his eyes. She leans over and, with deep hatred in her voice, whispers, "Maidaneck, Maidaneck." Jasinski shakes his head, his face as white as paper.

We help him on. He cannot walk, and the pain makes him glassy eyed. When we get him to the clearing, Kiedrzynska emerges from our group and softly slaps Jasinski's cheek, and the grimace of pain returns. "He is all right now," Kiedrzynska says, and we move him to the hole. It is deep and squared off. Kiedrzynska abandons ceremony and draws out the Walther P-38 that he took from a dead German officer, and pushes Jasinski into the hole. He screams, gripping his leg. I see by the way he lands that it is badly broken. Kiedrzynska waits, so that between screams he can say, "Yes, Maidaneck." The scream is louder. "Maidaneck!" Then he relieves the terrible pain in Jasinski's leg by shooting him once, in the top of his head. Another shot would be wasteful.

We must hurry to the other side of the village to wait. As we walk through, I pause by Katya's house. She has not been outside much in months because her husband and family are dead, her family in the Maidaneck camp, and her husband and twelve-year-old daughter hanged by the Germans—who got their information from Jasinski. They did it with very thin rope so that the necks were drawn bone tight, high under the jaws. I still see them turning slowly in the breeze.

Tonight is different. Katya is in the yard, using that same flat shovel to turn the soil for her garden. It is that time of year again. The wind molds her skirt against her fine legs, defining them in the delicate curves and sweeps of a classic statue. If we live through this, then youth will repeat itself; I will go to see her.

We hurry on to the other side of the village and sit, listening for the sound of motors and looking out over the plain into the twilight distance for the forms of the Russians on the eastern horizon.

TREBLINKA, EASTERN POLAND, SPRING 1945
Gold Rush

It is just after dawn. The boy has been digging for an hour, watched by his father, who believes anything of value will be buried shallowly among the trees adjacent to the ruins of the camp. The patches of dew-laden grass show their darker foottrails, which run next to holes already dug, "in places you'd be able to remember," the father had said, "next to a certain tree, or exactly between two trees."

The boy finishes a long, shallow hole and looks up with weary doubt at his father. "Nothing," he says.

The father muses, holding his chin. Then he looks at the mounded chunks of blasted cement and rusted billows of barbed wire fifty meters to their left. "Maybe we should try sifting the fire pit."

"What for?"

"It—there might be something."

"Who'd hide valuables in a fire pit?"

The father glares at the boy with a flash of anger and then looks back at the trees. "Let me think now, the guards would wander around here. Prisoners who gave them money for food or whatever would not be able to—now think, if you had something to hide, where would you bury it?"

"Over there?" the boy says, pointing toward the ruins.

"Fool! I told you there was a building there!" He rips the shovel from the boy's hands, his face wooden with rage. The boy stumbles back and says, "I'm sorry, I only—"

The father begins digging with furious concentration, flinging dirt with energy far in excess of need. The boy moves off, pretending to look for valuables. He kicks the sandy earth near a grassy bank, hoping that by some miracle this famous gold he has never seen will appear. Soon he is lost in a semiconscious swoon of vague expectation, kicking dirt out from under the grassy hummocks of the bank. His shoe strikes something hard and loosens the dirt. He continues kicking, then backs away. "Father!" His father turns as the boy points. It is the front half of a skull, lying on its side in the earth. The jaw is detached from the top, and the base of the skull is shattered, so that the interior looks like a little cave.

"The teeth!" the father says. "Look at the teeth!"

The boy gets down on his knees to look at the teeth—only five or six, no gold. Just as he is about to rise with the bad news, he senses movement inside the skull. He looks into the little cave, and in emerging definition he sees a mouse, standing above what look like four little blue-gray bullets—babies. "Oh, look!" he says. "Father, look here! Look!"

"What! What!" he snaps, walking quickly toward the boy.

"Look! It's mice, little baby mice! There's the mother! She has four babies—look!"

The father's face looks questioning for a moment, then darkens with rage and frustration. He raises the shovel and with four powerful whacks reduces the skull to fragments flattened into the earth. The boy watches, then turns toward the ruins of the camp. The air is blasted from his lungs, and he ends up on his face, his mouth full of dirt. At first he does not know what has happened, but then he sees his father looming over him, the shovel in his fist. Getting his breath back, the boy clears his mouth and stands up, the flat square of pain on his back increasing in intensity as his senses return. His father is digging again, now exactly between two trees.

BERLIN, MAY 1, 1945
The Father

The two young Waffen SS officers interrogated the old soldier and the two young conscripts near the doorway of a gutted bookstore. The air was thick with the smell of the muddy, blackened mounds of burned books inside. One SS officer pointed a Walther PPK at the three soldiers while the other asked questions in a sharp, rapid voice.

"Where are your weapons?"

The two young conscripts were ashen with fright, but the old man gazed back at the officers with fatigued contempt.

"A hundred kilometers back I found my village in ruins," he said in a soft, preoccupied voice. "My son is dead—"

"Answer my question!"

"—my wife is missing," he went on, "and they told me that my daughter—"

"Answer my question!"

"—who is only fourteen, set off on her own to the West."

The officer with the Walther pointed it at the old man.

"Our orders are to execute all deserters," the interrogator said.

The old man stood up, making the interrogator draw his pistol. Then he moved toward the doorway of the bookstore. "Yes, I saw some of your work back there," he said. "Boys hanging from trees. You swine, you worshippers of death."

"Stop!" the interrogator snapped. He turned to the other officer. "He's trying to draw you off from these two. Watch him."

"Swine," the old man said, "you're addicted to killing, you with your stupid tin death's-head. Go ahead."

"Where are your weapons?"

"I threw mine away, swine."

The officer's face flushed with anger, and he seemed to hover on the verge of firing.

"In the head, please," the old man said. He put his hand on his chest. "Down here's had enough."

"Where are your weapons?"

"Are you an imbecile?" the old man whispered with exaggerated curiosity. "I told you I threw mine away."

One of the young conscripts began to cry. The other looked numb and stared at a column of black smoke to his left.

The old man laughed, shaking his head. "Worshippers of death. Are you so stupid that you don't understand? Yes, I think this is why killers always seem so young. You are fed shit, and you smack your lips with pleasure, belch with satisfaction. Swine."

"Stop it!" the interrogator screamed. The hand holding the pistol began to tremble. The other officer holstered his Walther and walked up behind the interrogator. He reached around and removed the pistol from his hand. Suddenly the interrogator looked confused and, without the gun, incomplete, out of balance. The old man smiled.

"You're coming along with us," he said. "Both of you." He walked to the interrogator and removed his cap, revealing a head of fine, pale hair parted in the middle. He snapped the death's-head off the cap, dropped it on the ground and stepped on it, making a concave mask of the skull with the features drawn into the center. "We will have to dry you out, like a drunk," he said, "clean you of your addiction." The interrogator looked at him, still confused.

"Are you hungry?" the other officer asked the old man.

"Yes," he said. "It is kind of you."

They ate rations from the staff car. The old man looked at the officers and said, "We'll have to get you out of these preposterous uniforms." The officers looked down at themselves, then at each other. "And you," the old man said to the interrogator, "might you drive us to the Ruhr? Or shall we say Bielefeld? I would like to find my daughter."

The five soldiers got into the car.

"If we're caught we'll be shot," the interrogator said.

"Then I suggest we don't get caught," the old man said. "We'll surrender to the Americans. Mainly it's the cigarettes, I think; Russian cigarettes are terrible."

The interrogator started the engine and lurched the staff car violently, so that the old man laughed and looked at the others. "Onward to the ass of the fatherland," he said in a voice of pompous martial command.

The interrogator turned in his seat as he drove, again looking confused. "But isn't this treason?" he asked, as if it had not dawned on him until then.

NEAR BRUNSWICK, GERMANY, SPRING 1945
Poetic Justice

The two girls, both fourteen, walk two paces behind the town mayor Herr Wunsch. The American soldiers watch them pass, apparently angry about something. "What's the matter with him?" one girl asks in a whisper, passing a particularly sour-looking older soldier who is unshaven and rumpled looking. "Perhaps he is afflicted with acute constipation," the second girl whispers, and they both giggle, for a few moments so hard that they can barely control themselves, a problem that has caused them trouble in school.

The group is marched slowly, in pairs, to a wide, muddy path waffled with holes made by many feet and littered here and there with bits of rag, useless shoes, scraps of stained cardboard. The girls, wearing leather sandals, try to walk on the grassy edge, but one soldier holds out his rifle to keep them in line. "Oh, wonderful," one girl whispers. "The stupid savages! Look at my sandals!"

"Mine, too," the other girl says. "Pigs," she adds.

In the distance they see the townspeople looking down at what appears to be piles of rags, but, as they move closer, the girls see that they are bodies, many of them, resting in the muddy grass beside the path. The Americans ordering the people to look have white bands with red block crosses on their helmets.

Both girls are suddenly apprehensive. They must pass the long line of bodies and be forced to look. They approach the first ones—the faces gape, slack jawed, and the skin hangs in loose folds on the stick-thin limbs with the monstrously swollen joints. "It's *ugly*," one girl whispers. An American says something to her, pointing. Most of the corpses are women; some are bald; some are dressed in rags so shredded that the girls can see, inside the rips, flattened breasts hanging down over emaciated rib cages. They try not to look, but the Americans order them to look. "Oh, look there," one girl whispers. This corpse is a blonde girl whose mouth is not open. She looks almost as if she sleeps. "She doesn't look like a Jew," the girl whispers.

Finally they are past the line. The path goes on over a hillock. "I think it was one of those marches," one girl says. "My father said that people died on the marches." The other girl isn't listening. She is looking back angrily at an American soldier who stares with smug arrogance at her, chewing what appears to be tobacco. "Asshole," she says.

The American seems to know it is an insult. He taps another soldier on the back and asks him something, and the soldier shrugs. The girl begins to laugh. "What imbeciles," she whispers. "What stupid hulking animals!" The soldier steps toward her, smiling, then arcs a ball of brown spit at her. It lands in front of her feet, and droplets spatter her shins. The soldier laughs and turns away.

The girl is so livid with rage that when she turns to stomp off after the other villagers, she runs her big toe into a rock nestled in the grass. She sits in the grass and begins to cry, holding her muddy foot. From under the big toenail on her right foot, blood seeps into the caked mud on her sandal.

"Are you all right?" her friend asks.

"My nail is split! My shoes are ruined!" She continues to cry, rocking with the pain. "Why do they make us do this!" she shouts.

"Shh. Shh, don't."

"Savages! Stupid barbarians!" she yells, looking at the American soldier with scalding contempt, but he shrugs, then shifts that disgusting wad of tobacco from one cheek to the other.

BERLIN, MAY 1945
A Fair Hearing

Oberführer Janke held the pistol to his temple for ten seconds, his finger gently urging the trigger. Then he put it down and poured himself another cognac. Outside, only blocks away, he could hear them yelling, and he could hear occasional rifle fire. The lack of the sound of any heavier equipment meant the end. He felt his head rush with fatigue and a kind of moribund fright. Now, do it now. The thought that his city was being pillaged by the Russian savages had sunk into his awareness to the point where he had begun to wonder what would happen to the trivial mementoes on his desk: the marble bust of Schiller, the French miniature he had bought in Paris, the delicate figurines his wife had so cherished. His task of following her and the children now lay in wait, and, tears forming in his eyes, he wondered if this torture of playing with his suicide was worth the pain or was perhaps an insult to those who had so willingly obeyed his orders and approached death's threshold with such calm dignity. Yes, he should do it now. He picked up the pistol and studied it. Perhaps he would say one more good-bye. He rose from the desk and went to his bedroom.

His wife lay where he had shot her, her hands folded under her breasts. The wound in her temple had stopped leaking blood onto the bed. There was the edge of a urine stain where her skirt met the coverlet. He touched her arm and was momentarily surprised at how cold she was. Her lips were parted slightly, and he could see the one, off-color porcelain tooth she had had fixed a few years ago. He left her and went to the children's room. He decided not to touch them; since they had gone first, using tablets that she had said were "just some medicine," he knew they would be much colder than his wife. She had placed flattened wads of cotton on their eyes, and now they seemed only to be sleeping, except for the oddly contrasting patches of white; each was in the appropriate bed, hands folded. His son Peter had been suspicious, but then, at twelve, he had known more than the two little girls. Janke had been proud of his manly assurance, which this time had been mixed with the child's querulous and somewhat grudging obedience. You could see each of the two aspects in his bearing—the boy and the man. Janke thought he might cry again but decided he was weary of that indulgence and would now put himself to sleep and rejoin his family.

As he sat down at his study desk and again looked at the pistol, he heard the sounds of jubilant soldiers on the street below. So, it was time. He picked it up, placed the muzzle at his temple, and tensed himself. He remembered his orders: Fight to the last and save one bullet for yourself in a glorious gesture of exit. He wondered—perhaps he should fight, take some of those lower forms of life with him. A surge of vigorous willfulness suddenly electrified him. To fight, to deny just one or two of the foul animals their joy. Yes, he might do just that. He wondered—should he just wait for them? He sat at the desk.

When he heard the first of them kicking in the foyer door, he dropped the pistol into the waste basket and straightened his collar; he felt airy and glassy eyed with shock. An officer who seemed simply to appear before him addressed him in simple German. Janke stood up and faced the man. It was strange: He looked as Western as any Berliner and spoke with a nearly gentle softness. Two other soldiers briefly examined Janke's insignia and were for a moment somewhat excited. Janke was vaguely impressed by the simplicity of their uniforms.

As he was being led out, he caught, out of the corner of his eye, activity in the room where his wife lay. Two young soldiers had torn open the top of her dress and one had his hand on her bare left breast. Then he shook it vigorously and moved it in circles on her chest. The other soldier worked his hand under her skirt and then drew it out quickly and, laughing, wiped it on his pants. Janke had little reaction to this, only a stupefied curiosity. Other soldiers were peering into the children's room and whispering softly to each other.

Janke came to his senses when he found himself on the street. He looked at the officer and said, "I am not pleased with your unit's treatment of the dead."

The officer produced a sustained shrug as if to say, what can one do under the circumstances?

Then Janke drew himself up and said with forceful assurance, "I had nothing whatsoever to do with those camps! Nothing!" The officer shrugged again.

"I demand counsel!" Janke said. "According to the rules of war, I am entitled to a fair hearing!" When the officer shrugged again, Janke glared at him, thinking that it was no way for a man of his rank to behave.

NEAR STENDAL, GERMANY, SPRING 1945

Fallen Pin-up Girl

Hungerford sees him in there, sitting with his back against a wooden icebox under a section of corrugated roof. "Sind Sie Amerikaner oder Russe?"

"Out," Hungerford says, "uh, 'raus, schnell."

"Amerikaner—gut." He comes out—still fat, Hungerford sees, bald, thin little mustache. The German bows slightly, squinting in the light. He looks around, sees their other refugee, an ancient man in a black suit made gray by plaster dust. The two Germans seem to recognize each other.

Kelly still looks at the girl, who is untouched except for something that has nearly cut her in half at the waist. "Really looks a lot like Hayworth," Kelly says. "Ol' Rita up and down."

The fat German looks at the blackened shells of the buildings, his eyes watering. "So viele," he says. "Es ist schlecht, schlecht." Up along the gutter are more corpses, pushed out of the way so that the trucks could pass.

"Hey, Danny?" Kelly says. "Don't you think so? Like Hayworth?" The old German looks at the girl and at the fat man.

"Hey, Danny?" Kelly says.

"Sure," Hungerford says, "up and down."

The old German looks at the other bodies along the road. He becomes angry. He stumbles toward Hungerford and the fat one, gathering up his anger, and spits into the face of his countryman, who flushes and looks with shock at the aged face. The old man turns away, muttering.

"What got into him?" Kelly asks.

Hungerford shrugs and leads the fat German away. Wiping the spit from his face, the German says, "Schlecht." He has trouble seeing where he places his feet. The soft wind moves the hair on the girl's forehead.

NEAR ESSEN, SPRING 1945
Bad Dreams

Gretchen Beck has walked half the afternoon, carrying the small bag of belongings in one hand and holding her daughter's hand in the other. The child, walking two steps to her mother's one, clutches her doll and views the devastated villages with bright curiosity, while her mother averts her eyes from blackened buildings, overturned trucks, and occasional neat rows of prone bodies.

Every kilometer or so, they encounter more unshaven Americans, who search their belongings and wave them on, pointing in the direction of a village where a camp has been set up for refugees like herself.

"Mama!" She turns. The child laughs, holds the doll to her chest. Hanging by the neck from the splintered branch of a dead tree is a doll like her own, pink and smiling, but nude and without arms. It swings in the breeze, the black holes in its shoulders turning across their vision each time the head reaches its button-nosed profile. The child stares at it, the smile slowly passing from her face. Her mother shudders and pulls her along, feeling hunger twist in her stomach. She wonders how the girl can stand it.

The camp is a low metal-roofed building surrounded by a fence and tents. Inside, tired soldiers organize the aged, the women, and the children in lines before steaming pots of soup and mounds of hard bread. Gretchen cannot separate the child from the doll while they eat, and she reasons that, if it makes her secure, then it is all right. Watching the child, she thinks again of the loss of her husband and brother.

After twilight, they are given a single battered cot to sleep on. She is still hungry, but the child is at least exhausted enough to sleep. They lie nestled like spoons, the mother, child, and doll.

She orders dinner at a country Gasthaus. The proprietor, a fat Bavarian, shakes his head at her order of a simple meal and suggests the specialty of the evening with a cryptic, inarticulate speech. Even though it costs more, she nods, laughing. The meat is pale, swimming in a translucent butter sauce. He stands across the room nodding and gesturing, patting his stomach. Good, no? Yes, excellent! But the meat is too tender, too pale. When she cuts it, the flaccid, pale skin slides away and folds heavily into the sauce. Stunned, she realizes that it is the upper arm of a child. She drops her fork. . . .

Sweat trickles across her face. She rises to her elbows, breathing quickly. Across the building somewhere, an old man yells in his sleep. Her heart thumps and she trembles, trying to calm herself. Just as she lies down again, the child screams out, clutching at the blanket, at the air, then at the doll. She feels it, babbling shrill and urgent gibberish. "What?" her mother says. "What is it? What's the matter?" She holds the child's hands, then remembers. "Here," she says, "here, see? See? She has arms. Oh, yes! See the arms? Right here—see them? Oh, yes, she has arms."

BERLIN, SPRING 1945
Words and Pictures

The boy has rediscovered the attic. Standing in a dusty shaft of orange light, he looks around at the boxes and the trunks, vaguely remembering doing this three years ago before his parents had sent him to his grandmother's house in the country. He remembers his fingertips black with dust, remembers seeing old books, old watches with broken faces, old magazines and silken clothing that split at the slightest touch. His throat feels dry from breathing the dust, and, as he remembers, when his nose runs and he blows it, he will come away with phlegm tinged with flecks of blackish material. He steps toward the window, into better light.

He knows what is in that bundle on the floor and waits a moment to hear activity downstairs—yes, the rattling of pots in the kitchen and soft voices. His father is talking about the occupation again, speaking to her back while she prepares the pots. The boy stoops down to the bundle of magazines and carefully unties the string binding them together, trying to fix in his mind the way the knot is tied so that he can put it back after he has seen them. When he was five, he had felt a strange sensation of giddy, secret fascination in looking at the cartoons. He was sure that if his father had caught him looking, he would have been punished severely.

The first picture inside the magazine on top is of a pile of blond-haired children, each with a slit in the neck out of which spurts a single stream of blood, and the spurts of blood arc out and down into a dish held by two Jews wearing those little caps. Their dark, swollen lips protrude over their receded, unshaven chins, and their eyes look ferocious with a kind of lustful and evil pleasure. Their noses are huge with flared, black nostrils. In another picture, a hunchbacked Jew offers a little blonde girl candy, and in another the same Jew has his dirty hand on the heavy breast of a crying mother with braided hair, while in the other hand he holds what looks like a bag of money. In still another picture, two Jewish priests drain the blood from a dead baby's neck into a silver goblet. They do this with the appearance of great care, watching the blood with their deep-set eyes above the huge noses and the swollen lower lips. The caption calls them blood drinkers and rapists of children. The boy does not know what a rapist is. Deciding that he should not push his luck, he reties the knot over the magazine and leaves the attic, feeling a little dizzy and weak in the knees.

In the kitchen, his father sees his dirty hands. "What have you been doing?"

The boy is not sure if his three-year absence has changed his rights, at least in terms of what he is allowed to see. Suddenly he feels brave and says, "I was in the attic reading magazines."

"What magazines?" his father asks. Then he says to the boy's mother, "Things will settle down, I'm sure."

"That pile of magazines by the window—the ones with the pictures."

His mother turns and dries her hands on the two gray spots on her apron and places napkins on the table.

"We'll have to eat soon," she says. "Sundown's only an hour off, and then, except for the lamp, we're in the dark again."

"There's a whole big pile of them," the boy says.

"What?" his father says. "Oh, just don't alter the proper order of the issues."

"I won't," he says, backing out of the kitchen. He bounds up the stairs two at a time because there will be only a few more minutes of light.

BERLIN, SPRING 1945
Night Visit

Aichele sits in the dim candlelight, looking for the line from Rilke. He hears them coming, shouting, Frau, Frau! They will be in his house shortly. Still he looks for the line, his throat thickening with the familiar despair that is now tinged with a sense of mounting absurdity. Today he saw the Russians herding the new prisoners toward the camps. They were frightened, dirty boys, some pimply, all the same age as the ones he had once shooed away from his plum trees. The Führer is dead. Next door, Grubner's daughter, only fourteen, cowers in the bathroom, waiting for the Russians to pass. Aichele can see from his bedroom window upstairs that she hides there. He fears for her.

It was something like "Ich habe mein Glück und ich habe mein Weh und ich habe jedes allein." He tires, flipping the pages. His luck and his grief. All alone. Upstairs his wife and daughter lie under a quilt on the floor, their fronts untouched as if they sleep, and their backs blasted, punctured with thick splinters of wood from the force of the shattering wall against which they had sat, trembling, during the bombing two days ago. He has requested help to remove them and is indignant at the absence of propriety concerning burial.

Now on the porch, Frau, Frau! He rises, thinking, only a short time ago, on the Potsdamer Platz, there were English poets, German intellectuals, women. . . . He opens the door. They smile without malice. What victor needs to display it? One has malevolent Kirghiz eyes, not unlike Elizabeth's. Aichele backs away and permits them to enter. They look around. He smells liquor on their breath. Aichele points to the stairs, and they stamp up, disregarding the ancient rug that is threadbare in the middle from a million former steps. Aichele winces.

He follows, holding the candle high and placing his feet on the thicker edges of the carpet as he has done for many years. The two soldiers see the covered forms in the candlelight, which casts moving shadows on the wall from Aichele's unsteady hand. The air is touched with the odor of their decomposition, which is just beginning. One soldier falls to his knees and uncovers them. He crosses himself, rises. The soldiers cross themselves again and utter brief prayers. The one with the Kirghiz eyes pats Aichele on the shoulder and looks gravely at his face. They depart, leaving him staring down at the still forms of his wife and daughter.

The Russians continue down the street, saying, Frau, Frau! They find the Grubner girl. It is as if they had known always that she would be there. *How horrible!* he thinks. They do not bother to blow out the candle. She only cries, does not fight. Aichele steps to the window, now that they have found her. His candle dulls his vision, so he blows it out and looks down into the little soft orange rectangle of window at the hunched forms of the soldiers.

EAST OF THE ELBE RIVER, MAY 1945

An Application of Logic

Conscript Wilhelm Krass stands at attention, awaiting his commanding officer's orders. With his back to him, Standartenführer Ehlert carefully places the deserters' papers in the canvas-covered bed of the truck, in a wooden box holding rolls of undeveloped film. He has explained to Krass that, despite the need for accurate recording, he has decided not to photograph the deserters. A simple listing will do, along with a report of the executions. He arranges the film rolls in the box to make space for the expanding wad of identity papers and orders.

"Later you will alphabetize these for me," Ehlert says.

"Yes, oberst."

Krass, who is seventeen, had joined them two weeks ago after having recovered from a minor wound; he now feels paralyzed inside a nightmare. The war is over, yet Standartenführer Ehlert continues to execute German soldiers, with such casual ease that Krass fears that one mistake might mean his joining the collections of records in the box. Worse, Ehlert is too smart for the Russians to catch, or for Krass to run from.

Ehlert leans out of the covered truck bed into the bright light and looks off to the left where two of the men are hanging the third deserter, an old Scharführer who was the one who had walked up to Ehlert and announced that the war was long over and that there was no need to worry anymore about uniforms. The entire German army had surrendered, he said. He and his companions were going to the Elbe, to the Americans. Ehlert explained to him that he had received no orders that contradicted those by which he had been operating; it made no difference to him how many soldiers of the Reich were left. He looked around and pointed out that, counting himself, there were at least five. By what logic, then, could one assert that there has been a total surrender? He then shot the old Scharführer's two companions and told him that, according to tradition, the Scharführer himself would be hanged. Throughout this, Krass had observed Ehlert's men, who in their mysterious silence had seemed to show their declining tolerance for his madness. It was only a matter of time.

Because there is nothing left nearby more than a meter and a half tall, the men have attached the noose rope to a tree stump and are pulling the old Scharführer away from it by his feet, so that he is horizontal to the ground. Straining each to a leg, the men lean at sharp angles as they struggle for footing. The Scharführer's face is grotesquely contorted, and his lips are purple. Then the air is tinged with the odor of voided bowels. "Another thirty seconds," Ehlert says to Krass.

"Yes, oberst."

Beyond the men, the third member of Ehlert's unit goes through the packs of the other two deserters.

When the execution is finished, and Ehlert's men drag the body a few meters away to join those of the other deserters, Krass is aware that they are whispering to each other about something. Hauser, second in command, looks once in Ehlert's direction, and Krass begins to tremble. The men now approach the truck. They appear to be snickering about something. Krass thinks, now, they'll do it now. They'll put a stop to this now.

"Please," Hauser says to Ehlert. "Here, sit on the running board." Ehlert cocks his head at him, then shrugs.

"Certainly," he says. "Is everything complete?"

"Not quite," Hauser says. Ehlert sits, and Hauser reaches into his pocket. Krass stands back, holding his breath.

"Behold!" Hauser says. "Shoe polish!"

He gets down on his knees and goes to work on Ehlert's shoes.

"There's a bottle of schnapps in the back," Ehlert says softly. "Later we'll pass it around."

When Hauser finishes Ehlert's shoes, he stands up, winded from the vigor of his work. Ehlert studies them briefly.

"Come look," he says.

His heart thumping, Krass steps over and leans down, and he stares into the brilliant leather, which in the sun shows the tiny, warped reflections of himself and the other men.

Ehlert sighs and slaps his knee. "Well, gentlemen," he says, "we shall rest a little, before we hide."

There is a long silence; Krass fears long silences. "Shall I arrange the records now, oberst?" he asks.

NEAR KASSEL, GERMANY, SUMMER 1945
Repatriation

During this first day of his return, Wirtz is continually amazed that little, if anything, has changed: There, above the black stove, are the shiny pots, and above them the little clock he had bought for her in Berlin. He believes that it is because of some mystical luck that his wife and house have been spared. The Russians did not come beyond the Elbe, only a hundred kilometers to the east, and the Americans only passed by, scanning the countryside from their gun turrets and jeeps, leaving only cleat tracks in the fields. Wirtz had made the last leg of his journey home wearing a regular army uniform taken from a dead soldier in eastern Germany. He had discarded his own, which would have identified him as one of the SS and hence worth interrogating. It had all seemed to him almost too simple until this morning, when his wife had admitted that, having assumed he had been killed, she had become involved with another man, a soldier healing from wounds taken in the Stalingrad battle.

She now enters the kitchen silently, carrying a plate piled up with small beet greens, young shoots from sweet potato plants, and two eggs. As he watches her, he wonders about the meaning of having been spared, as if there must be some message in it; so many have died, after all. Then perhaps her lack of faith in him is equitable punishment for his deeds: He had shot German soldiers who ran like cowards from the Russians. On orders, of course, but, after days of carrying out these orders, of watching his countrymen flop onto the ground as he holstered his pistol, Wirtz had found himself deserting in a dead man's uniform. From then on, he knew that his life would be different.

Now he must sit and envision his wife naked under that soldier. Everything has become ironic. He had thought that great spans of time would be spent atoning for the executions he had carried out, but now that is all replaced by an endless string of images of his wife and the soldier, who, because he is faceless, will have all faces, even those of the men he executed.

Supper is meager, yet it satisfies him. Shortages are to be expected. Soon, after dusk, they prepare for bed. He undresses silently while she brushes her hair with long, outward thrusts of her arm. The dying light penetrates the soft cloth of her nightgown, making his heart thump in anticipation. She has barely even lost weight. She turns and approaches the bed with caution, eyes showing that she awaits his judgment. He stands, and then on an impulse strikes her once, hard, on the side of the head. She gasps and staggers back, shocked, knocking a little bisque figurine of a dancer to the floor. It shatters in a quickly expanding circle of curved pieces, like seashells. When she sees the bright pieces, her eyes flood. He stares down at the broken figurine, vaguely recalling buying it for her. Where? Munich, perhaps. It was a day in late spring. He suddenly feels melancholy and tired but happy that it is over and that they are safe. "Let us say only that we thank God we have been spared," he says.

MESSINGHAUSEN, GERMANY, SUMMER 1945
The Unknown Soldier Passes

Irmhild Stauffer walks down the dusty Messinghausen street, lugging in her right hand the heavy container of milk and seeing by her shadow that her body is offset by its weight; it seems to her that she has passed the entire war listening to her own footfalls. Only once did she see troops passing. And to where? She could not remember the direction. Brilon, to the north, where nothing of any value could be contested? Niedermarsburg to the south, where nothing of any value existed either? So went the first war, too. Her husband, children, all had gone off, the men to die in both wars, and her daughter doubtless to a more sinful end in Duisburg.

She walks in the opposite direction from the current of the stream that runs along the railroad tracks, through the gorge from Brilon. She sees the little crowd coming in her direction, pointing down at the water, the men talking, the women covering their faces and retreating to the other side of the road. Some object in the water draws them along, makes the crowd increase in size as it approaches her. Old Müller, who, forty years ago, was almost her lover, maintains his stern gait in the effort of walking so fast and gestures at the sky with his cane.

She puts the can down. The object, she sees now, is an arm, with a military sleeve tightly containing it and a bloated hand traveling always palm up, whirling slowly in the gentle eddies like a small ship in a sea storm. She stands still and lets the crowd pass, streaming by her. Müller's cane brushes against her skirt. They continue on, discussing the bloated arm as it goes on its southward journey. She picks up the can and continues toward her house. When she reaches it, aching from the effort, she stands on the porch and watches the crowd, which is now nearly twice the size of the one that briefly engulfed her a minute ago. It follows the arm out the other end of town. She leaves the milk on the porch and goes into the house to look, with close attention, at each of the many photographs of her husband and sons.

Design by David Bullen
Typeset in Mergenthaler Ehrhardt
by Wilsted & Taylor
Printed by Haddon Craftsmen
on acid-free paper

MERCYHURST COLLEGE
HAMMERMILL LIBRARY
ERIE, PA 16546